H

The Shadow
of Suspicion

Also Available in Large Print
by Emilie Loring:

A Key to Many Doors

EMILIE LORING

THE SHADOW OF SUSPICION

G.K.HALL &CO.

Boston, Massachusetts

1982

Library of Congress Cataloging in Publication Data

Loring, Emilie Baker.
  The shadow of suspicion.

  "Published in large print"--Verso t.p.
  1. Large type books. I. Title.
[PS3523.O645S5 1982]   813'.52   82-6075
ISBN 0-8161-3395-6   AACR2

Published in Large Print by arrangement with
Little, Brown and Company.

Set in 18 pt Times Roman

The Shadow
of Suspicion

I

NEW YORK on a December night. A light snow falling, muting the sounds of traffic, dimming the brilliant red and green of traffic lights, falling like a diaphanous wedding veil in front of the magnificent windows of the Fifth Avenue shops.

In the windows wax figures postured in evening gowns, in fabulous furs, in flimsy negligees, in exquisite jewels, while holly boxes, elaborate wrapping paper and ribbon in the background suggested that these glamorous objects would delight some woman.

The man who had paused before one of the windows was tall, broad-shouldered and slim-hipped. Brows that nearly met, clear gray eyes that looked out of a bronzed face . . . He had the mouth of a man of temper kept rigidly under control. In spite of the hurry, the excitement in the air, the electric movement of Fifth Avenue, the bustle of Christmas shopping, many women looked and turned to look again at Don Bruce, captivated as much by his indifference, his unawareness, as by his virile good looks.

Taxis jostled private cars, buses were jammed with laughing crowds, their arms piled high with gaily wrapped packages. Horns sounded, motors throbbed, heels clicked over the pavements. Everything moved fast, faster, as though on a mad race toward some unseen goal.

New York, Don Bruce thought, and took a long breath. After the world he had come from it seemed unbelievable. He had forgotten it was so beautiful, sparkling, arrogant, prosperous. And promising, he thought. A place of hope, of aspiration. And most beautiful now, at Christmas.

For the first time in weeks he was aware of a surge of optimism, of renewed faith in himself. He had a soaring belief that, after all, in spite of what seemed to be insurmountable obstacles, he would pull it off. All these weeks he had grown more and more convinced that the Bruce luck had failed him at the time when he needed it most. Ever since he had lost the trail he had followed over thousands of miles, over months of time, he had been increasingly discouraged. It had seemed to him that there was literally no place left to go, no clue left to follow. And yet, through it all, he had been aware of a kind of hunch, a sense of hurry, something goading at him, warning him, ''There's no time to lose.''

Perhaps, he thought, it was the spirit of Christmas in the air that was reviving the hope that had almost been extinguished.

At the corner of Fifth Avenue and Fiftieth Street, a bearded Santa Claus stamped his feet on the icy sidewalk and jingled his bell. Don Bruce removed his furlined glove and felt in his pocket for coins which he dropped into the meshed top of the kettle standing on its tripod.

''Cold work,'' he said, white teeth gleaming in his bronze face as he smiled at the man in the red suit and false beard, who shivered as a gale blew down the street.

''Nice work though, sir,'' the man replied. ''A time when people are giving to

3

others. Even when my hands get cold it warms me, somehow.''

Don stripped off the other glove and forced them both into the chilled hands of the surprised Santa Claus. ''No reason why your hands shouldn't be as warm as your heart,'' he said gruffly and crossed Fifth Avenue in haste to escape the man's fervent thanks.

He glanced at his watch. Only six o'clock. Too early for dinner. He walked with long strides toward Broadway, a man accustomed to action, restless because there was no clear course open to him. Automatically, he swept each face he passed with searching eyes, though he was bitterly aware that looking for the one face he sought among New York's millions was like the proverbial search for a needle in a haystack.

And there was no reason to believe that the man he wanted so desperately to find was in New York. He might be at the ends of the earth by now. There was not even a reason to believe that he would recognize him if he did see him. What did he have to go on, after all? Only a few phrases spoken in a tone too low to recognize, a view of a man's back so hunched over that he could not even determine his height and build.

When he reached Broadway, Don stood — while snowflakes brushed his face with light, cool fingers — looking at the gaudy signs that flashed on and off, watching the crowds, hearing laughter, seeing people who talked unafraid, who walked without looking over their shoulders.

Always two, he thought. A girl and a boy, a young couple laughing as they tried to maneuver a gigantic toy through the mob, an elderly couple clinging together so they would not be separated by the noisy, shoving throng. Always two. But he had to go on alone until his self-appointed task was completed. If it ever was. There was no place for a woman in this wandering life of his. Even if he could find a woman whom he would be able to love completely. So far he hadn't.

At length he strolled back toward Rockefeller Center where the great Christmas tree soared up into the sky. The muted sound of Christmas carols drifted from the loudspeaker in a Fifth Avenue store window. Don leaned on the rail and watched the skating rink below where, to the strains of the "Blue Danube" waltz, figures skimmed and leaped and whirled. Professional skaters did exhibition steps, young couples with linked arms waltzed to the music, teen-age boys raced around the edges at top speed, an elderly man wearing a long black overcoat, his hands clapsed behind his back, skated slowly around the rink as though he were out for an afternoon stroll, seeming absorbed in his thoughts, but ably skirting the other skaters without collision.

On impulse, Don went down the steps and entered one of the restaurants whose glass walls provided a sheltered spectator's box for the skating. The room seemed unexpectedly warm after the cold air. He checked overcoat, hat, and muffler, felt for his gloves and remembered that he had given them away to the shivering Santa Claus.

The head waiter, practiced at summing up the importance of his customers, gave him a keen glance, looked around and made a gesture. All the tables near the glass wall beside the ice rink were occupied but, at his signal, a waiter hastily brought a small table and fitted it into the last remaining bit of space.

When Don had ordered he glanced

around, recognizing faces. A well-known columnist, an aging but still lovely actress, a musician whom Don had once traveled miles to hear play the violin to men shivering in a Quonset hut, bringing them for an hour the gift of beauty. Where could you find all this but in New York? He turned to look at the swirling figures on the rink, dipping, whirling, leaping, gliding.

Not until the first course arrived did he turn back to the room, pick up his napkin, and look straight into the girl's eyes.

ii

She was facing him at the next table. She was, he thought, the loveliest thing he had ever seen. Near-black hair waved softly above a triangular face with a broad forehead and pointed chin. Eyes like black velvet pansies looked out from under long lashes. He had known more beautiful women. What was it that set her apart, that gave her a kind of glow? Some inner zest, he thought, a deep-lying love of life.

Then the sparkle was gone from her eyes, which became wider, startled. A

7

soft flush crept up over her cheeks to her forehead. She turned away abruptly and Don realized that all this time he had been staring at her and she at him.

He devoted himself to his dinner, but he had forgotten the skaters swirling past the window on his left. He was aware only of the girl at the next table. Now and then he risked a quick look. She was in her early twenties, he thought, with a dewy freshness in the clear eyes and the beautiful skin that was like a young child's. Something untouched, something easily hurt, something to be treasured and protected. Yet — something valiant, that would never attempt to cling . . .

He tried to laugh at himself. You can't afford to get sentimental over a strange girl whom you'll never see again, he reminded himself. It didn't help, sensible as the warning was. In a few moments he seemed to have gone beyond the reach of sense, beyond caution. The thought of leaving the restaurant without knowing her identity was like pain.

Her green velvet dinner dress left her creamy shoulders and arms bare. Over the back of the chair hung a black velvet cape lined with sable. She lifted her left hand

and Don caught the gleam of an emerald on her fourth finger. His heart gave a jolt.

What did you expect, man? Someone was bound to capture a girl like that. Did you think she'd be waiting for you to come along? And what does it matter to you? You've never seen her before. You'll never see her again. And you have a job to do. Remember? A job that leaves no place for a woman in your life.

Nevertheless, his imagination had got out of control. While he ate his dinner he let himself imagine what it would be like to have her across the table from him, sharing his experiences; to have her to come home to when the job was done — if it was ever done. He had sworn that he would not give up until he had accomplished what he had set out to do. That was in the days — up to four months earlier — when he had believed in the Bruce luck.

There were two men with the girl in the green dress. The elderly man was small and thin, with a narrow distinguished face and a low cultivated voice that held an undertone of authority. This was a man who was so accustomed to being listened to that he had never found it necessary to raise his voice. Bruce looked at him, frowning. The man's face was familiar but he could not place him. The younger man was tall and assured, with a somewhat stiff manner. He was probably the fiancé, Don thought. He had always regarded himself as being both cool and detached in forming his judgments, so it was a surprise to discover that he disliked the young man extremely. I'm jealous, he realized. This is the most ridiculous thing I've ever done. It's high time I got myself under control.

Without intending to do so, he had so concentrated his attention on the next table that he could hear the low-pitched conversation above the louder talk at other tables, above the strains of the "Merry Widow" waltz now playing for the skaters.

It was the girl's voice he heard first, soft but eager. "You said you had something to tell me, Mr. Brewster, and I'm sure it's about Aunt Deb. Why on earth is she spending the winter in the Maine woods? She promised to help me with my trousseau and the wedding plans."

Brewster. Click. The name fell into place in Don's memory. No wonder the small man with the distinguished face had seemed familiar! Newton Brewster, famous corporation lawyer now retired, adviser to presidents. President maker, some said. A great and useful but anonymous citizen. "Everyone," Bruce had been told in Washington, only the week before, "goes to Brewster for advice. I don't know how he does it but he always comes up with something helpful, if it's only to act as a morale builder."

Brewster looked perplexed now, not like a man with a ready-made solution. "You're right, Julie. I've just come back from a visit to your Aunt Deb in Maine."

Julie, Don thought. I know that much about her, anyhow.

"I knew it," the girl exclaimed. "How is she?"

"I'm worried about your aunt," Brewster said. "She shouldn't be there. I did my best to persuade her to come back to New York but she had made up her mind." He flung out his hand in a helpless gesture.

The girl gave a little ripple of laughter. "I know Aunt Deb when she has made up her mind. An avalanche wouldn't budge her."

11

"That," remarked the younger man, "is where you resemble her, Julie."

She smiled at him mischievously. "What you should have, Quentin," she declared, "is a girl like soft wax so you can mold her into your pattern."

"Not at all," Quentin said stiffly. Quentin, Don decided, did not like being joked with. What sort of life companion would he make for the girl in whom laughter bubbled like champagne? "But once you make up your mind, Julie, you go your own way. You'll have to admit that. At times, you are darned stubborn."

The girl turned to the older man, the brightness fading from her face. "Aunt Deb has never stayed through the winter before. While Uncle Jim was alive they went up to the lodge for the hunting but she always came back to New York for the winter season. She loves the shops and theaters and art galleries and concerts. After Uncle Jim's death last fall she planned to sell the place rather than go there without him. Anyhow, she has a bad heart." The girl's voice trembled. Steadied. "Why is she staying?"

Brewster cleared his throat. "We all imagined that Jim Blaine was in more than

12

easy circumstances, but it turns out that he was in financial difficulties when he died. He left a lot of debts. Unless they can be paid by spring, your aunt will be penniless. I tried . . .'' There was a pause and then Brewster smiled, a warm smile that softened the austerity of his face. ''Of course, I've been in love with your aunt all my life but I never seem to learn that there is but one man for her. . . . Anyhow, she won't let me help.''

''But what,'' Quentin asked, ''does she hope to accomplish up there?''

''She is determined to have enough timber cut for pulp to meet Jim's debts. And she could do it, too, and save the estate — if things went smoothly.''

''But why,'' Quentin said in a disapproving voice, ''should she stay there herself? After all, *she* can't very well cut timber.''

''Well,'' Brewster replied, ''the situation is rather complicated. If her manager had lived, things would probably be all right. But he was killed a month ago in a hunting accident. Since then the crew of men has been raising a lot of trouble. They have to be supervised all the time to keep them on the job. Your aunt has some supervisors, but several of them are married and their wives refused to stay up there for the winter. As a result, the supervisors said they would not stay without their wives. So your Aunt Deb has turned the lodge into a sort of inn where the wives have pleasant rooms and excellent meals and whatever luxuries the woods can provide. She is acting as a kind of hostess to keep them contented.''

''That's absurd,'' Quentin said decisively. ''She should fire the superintendents and hire some men who won't demand the impossible.''

''That brings up another problem,'' Brewster said with a wry smile. ''Deborah Blaine feels that the noncombatant owes a great debt to men who have seen the bitterest part of actual warfare. And an even greater debt to men who were imprisoned by the Reds and had additional suffering of mind and body. So she has taken as her superintendents the men about whom there were stories in the papers a few months ago, some Communist prisoners in Korea who were finally released. She wants to give them a break.''

"Sentimental," scoffed the young man.

"Oh, Quentin," Julie protested. "The poor fellows! I understand how she feels."

"It's all right to feel sorry, Julie, but your aunt happens to need competent men."

"So far as that goes," Brewster said slowly, "they are all competent men: Swen Oorth, Curtis Wheeler, Charlie Keane and Hugh Gordon. I met them while I was there."

"You said, 'So far as that goes,' " Julie prompted him quickly. "Something more is troubling you."

"Something I feel." Brewster hesitated. "Not facts. I don't like it. I wish to heaven I could find a topnotch man to replace her manager. If she won't leave, at least there should be someone on hand to take over the responsibility, shoulder the burden, and handle the disgruntled men and a situation as tricky as a time fuse. The atmosphere is all wrong. There's tension. Hard feeling. Hostility. All the ingredients are there for battle, murder, and sudden death."

Sudden death. The words jarred. Out

15

of place among the skaters. Out of place in this Christmas season. But for Don there was exhilaration. The Bruce luck, he thought exultantly. The Bruce luck! I lose the trail in a back-street restaurant in San Francisco's Chinatown and I pick it up in a New York restaurant three thousand miles away.

He was so engrossed in his thoughts that temporarily he lost track of the conversation he had been following with such breathless interest. He was brought up to alert attention when he heard the man called Quentin say sharply, "No! I won't have it, Julie."

The girl's eyes snapped. "It's no use, Quentin," she said crisply. "Aunt Deb feels she has to stay there, but with her weak heart she needs someone with her. I'm going."

"I forbid it," he said.

Unexpectedly, the girl laughed. "Don't be absurd! After all, I'm free and twenty-four."

"You aren't free," he said obstinately. "You are engaged to me. We're to be married in April and there are a dozen functions already planned for us during the winter season as well as the apartment still to furnish. Anyhow, I won't allow you to do a ridiculous thing like this, chasing off into the Maine woods among a lot of roughnecks. You'll stay right here and go ahead with your plans.''

The girl looked at him incredulously. ''We don't seem to be tuned in on the same wave length,'' she said at last. ''I thought marriage was a partnership, not a master-and-slave relationship. I thought it was a sharing. I don't mean that we ought to agree on everything, but at least we ought to respect each other's opinions. Each other's conscience. You're too arrogant, Quentin. You — trample. And you lack respect.''

He laughed in a way that was guaranteed to irritate any woman. ''Don't be childish, darling. I know best and you'll have to accept my judgment.'' As she remained silent, he added, ''My fiancée won't go to the Maine woods. That's final.''

There was a gleam of green light as the girl pulled off the emerald ring and pushed it across the table. ''Julie Ames goes,'' she said.

''My dear Julie — Quentin,'' Brewster said in consternation, ''you don't realize what you are doing. Let's not be hasty over something that has nothing to do with your engagement.''

Don saw that the girl had become very pale but her chin was high, the soft mouth unexpectedly firm. ''It has everything to do with it. A marriage without respect isn't worth having.''

''Darling,'' Quentin protested in bewilderment, ''you know I'd give you anything —''

''Anything — but freedom to make up my mind and come to my own decisions,'' she smiled forlornly.

''You must learn to accept my judgment, Julie. And we are still engaged. We'll be married right on schedule. You need someone to direct your life for you.''

The waiter brought Don's check. He paid it, stood up. As he did so the three at the next table glanced at him. He did not look their way. It wasn't necessary. He knew now that, with the Bruce luck, he'd be seeing the girl again.

As he stopped to slip a bill into the head waiter's hand he faced the mirrored wall across the restaurant. In it he saw Brewster's eyes fixed on his face for a startled moment. Saw recognition. Speculation.

"The fellow looks a bit like a buccaneer," Quentin remarked disparagingly and Don swallowed a laugh. Quentin disliked him instinctively just as he disliked Quentin. Though no words had been exchanged, they knew that they were rivals. "He reminds me of those old Douglas Fairbanks movies, laughing while he's up to devilment. Probably an actor."

"That," Brewster remarked in his low, deliberate voice, "is a dangerous man. A very dangerous man."

Don Bruce smiled grimly to himself. So Brewster knew who he was. In the long run that might be helpful. He couldn't ask for a better ally. He left the restaurant and went in search of a telephone booth, where he dialed Western Union and sent a telegram.

II

THERE WAS a long mournful whistle as the train approached the town. It sounded almost like a scream of warning: *"Look out! Look . . . out!"*

Julie Ames shivered. All of a sudden she was aware that she did not want to leave the warmth and security of the Pullman. She wanted to go back to New York, back to Quentin — even if he would look superior and say, "I told you so" — back to her plans for the approaching wedding and the parties and the decoration of the duplex apartment which Quentin had taken on a five-year lease. It was larger than she would have chosen for herself but he did not think of consulting her taste.

She had pretended to be delighted but she had felt a pang of disappointment. A duplex penthouse on the East River with a curving marble stairway, a terrace that extended around three sides, a view of the busy river and a breath-taking panorama of the city itself. Anyone should be delighted, she had scolded herself. But her dream of a small house in the country had died hard.

Now she wondered why she had objected to the penthouse. Nothing could have hurt her there. She would have been surrounded by safeguards and people. Not a lonely, empty landscape, not a desolate train whistle like a somber warning.

Take a long breath and stop having such fancies, she scolded herself. The train screeched around a curve. What's the matter with me, the girl wondered. I've never been morbid before. It's all Quentin's warnings, his forebodings. I've been taking them too seriously.

But it wasn't simply Quentin, she realized. What disturbed her more than anything was the telephone call from Newton Brewster before she left New York.

''Are you still planning to go to Maine?'' he had asked her.

''Of course.''

There had been a long pause and then

21

he had said, "I wish you wouldn't go, Julie."

"But why? You are worried about Aunt Deb yourself. You agreed that she should have someone with her."

"I can't explain. But I urge you to stay where you are."

"Mr. Brewster," she had asked in alarm, "is there something you haven't told me?"

"The situation there is — unsettled," he had said evasively. "I'll be uneasy about you."

"If Aunt Deb can take it, I can," she had assured him gaily.

"Another thing, I really think you ought to pay more attention to Quentin's wishes, my dear. After all, it is only natural that he should be reluctant to have you run any risks. And your aunt will be awfully upset if she finds out that you broke your engagement on her account."

"But I didn't," Julie assured him. "I realized — oh, I should have known sooner, of course — that we don't seem to value the same things. Aunt Deb isn't in the least to blame."

In the rush of canceling arrangements with dressmakers, breaking appointments

22

with her friends, avoiding Quentin's angry telephone calls, and packing for her trip, Julie had let Brewster's warning sink into the back of her mind. But now she could no longer evade it.

For the first time in her young life she felt utterly alone, cut off from people, from her friends, from help. If only Quentin had understood, had sympathized. But he would not listen. And so the quarrel had ended in a broken engagement. Not that Quentin had accepted her decision as final.

''You'll come back,'' he had said with the assurance that irritated her. ''If you don't, I'll come for you. But we'll be married in April — according to schedule.''

Julie had known Quentin Harrington since she was five years old. He had always been there, playing with her as a small child, teaching her to swim and play tennis and golf, to drive her first car, to ride horseback, to sail a boat. Everyone had assumed that they would marry. When he finally proposed — and she stifled a giggle when she thought that he had probably done it according to schedule — her answer had been taken for granted.

It had never occurred to her to ask herself whether she loved him, whether his
companionship was necessary to her happiness or whether it was merely a habit,
whether their opinions and beliefs and
values were similar enough for harmony.

And now she was alone. For a moment
she felt a sharp longing for him and then
a chilly thought struck her. Even if he
were here, he wouldn't understand. I'd
still be alone.

She thought of his face, unrelenting,
uncompromising, impatient, closed to her
pleas. And beside it a man's clear gray
eyes under brows that nearly met. Eyes
that had looked into her very heart,
deeply, deeply. A tingle went along her
nerves but this time there was no chill of
fear; this was a warm glow. After that
first startled awareness that they had been
staring like — like strangers who recognized each other, she had been careful not
to look his way again. Until he had risen
to go and she had risked a glance at him.

He looked like a buccaneer, Quentin
had sneered. He was a man of action,
there was no doubt of that. With laughter
in his eyes and tenderness in his mouth
and strength. A man to be reckoned with.

A dangerous man, Mr. Brewster had said. *A very dangerous man.*

He was just an exceptionally handsome man in a restaurant, Julie told herself firmly. A stranger whom you'll never see again. Forget him.

She peered through the window of the slowly moving train. A heavy curtain of snow shut out the landscape. It seemed to her that there was nothing outside but the white blanket of snow and howling wind. Never before had she been here in midwinter. She had usually come up for a week during the hunting season when the Blaines opened their lodge, but it had never been like this. Even in the over-heated Pullman she shivered, pulled a fur-lined cap of red velvet down over her dark hair, over her ears, drew on fur-lined gloves, made sure the collar of her coat was turned high around her throat, and followed the porter down the swaying car to the exit.

The train jolted to a stop, the porter opened the door and got out the step. Air like ice rushed in, bit into Julie's face, cut off her breath. With the porter's help she went down the step and off into deep snow, whose frozen crust crackled as her feet sank through. The shivering porter hastily set down her luggage, pocketed her tip, and after a wave of his arm, put the step inside. The door closed, the engine jolted, moved slowly, faster, the whistle screaming as the train pulled away from the station, gathering speed.

Looking up, Julie saw that most of the windows were still curtained. It was not yet eight o'clock. She was the only passenger to get off. She felt a half-crazy impulse to hail the moving train, to get on and ride away, anywhere.

Huddled in her coat, blinking away the snowflakes that clung to her long lashes, she turned around facing the full force of the wind. She was at the end of a long platform covered by a drift of snow. There were no prints on that unbroken white surface. I'd feel like Robinson Crusoe if I saw a footprint, she laughed to herself. At the other end of the wooden platform was a red stationhouse. From a leaden sky snow fell in a heavy, blinding curtain. Beyond, she could make out a small cluster of houses.

Knee deep in the frozen snow she became aware that her legs were getting numb with cold. Hadn't the porter said it was fifteen below zero? She'd freeze if she stayed here any longer. She'd turn into the Ice Maiden.

Julie burrowed her chin into her collar and started for the station, pulling one foot out of the snow, plunging in again. The burning cold of the snow, the icy crust, hurt her legs as she plowed painfully ahead, half bent over against the gale-force of the wind that drove icy particles into her cheeks and her eyes. No use trying to handle her luggage by herself. She'd have to leave it in the snow. Surely Aunt Deb would send someone to meet her. The camp was over a mile from the village.

A man came out of the station, wearing a duffel coat, stocking cap and high boots. He picked up the mail sack which had been tossed off the train and started back into the station, dragging the sack over the snow. He paid no attention to Julie though he must have seen her, the only moving figure in all that white, frozen landscape.

Anger spurred her on and she reached the door at last, fumbled at the round knob with hands that had almost lost feeling. Stumbled inside.

It was a station like tens of thousands scattered through the more remote sections of America, a dingy frame structure, not too clean — with a few wooden benches, a scattering of orange peels and gum wrappers and cigarette butts — a counter, behind which the stationmaster had gone. The window was pulled down. He paid no attention to her. In the middle of the room was a pot-bellied stove, its sides glowing with heat. Julie started toward it. The stationmaster flung up the window.

"Hey, don't get too close until you've warmed up a little."

"Th-thanks," Julie said through chattering teeth. "Has anyone come to meet —" She broke off because he had slammed the window down again. Through it she could hear the ticking of the telegraph.

What's wrong with the man, Julie wondered in bewilderment. Never before had anyone refused so rudely to answer her appeal, to come to her assistance. What's the matter? She shook snow off her coat, knocked her shoes together, stamped her feet to help restore circulation. And all the time she was thinking: What's wrong?

Because something is terribly wrong. There can't be more than two hundred people in this village. That man handled my telegram to Aunt Deb. He must know who I am. Then why . . .

She hated to leave the comfort of the stove but she crossed the cold station, went to the window, tapped on it. Reluctantly the stationmaster raised it. ''Well?'' he said.

''I've come to visit Mrs. Blaine,'' Julie told him.

He had a narrow face, a long nose, long chin, the melancholy expression of a bloodhound. His thin mouth tightened. He watched her with open hostility. ''What am I supposed to do?'' he asked nastily. ''Cheer?''

Julie's face burned. ''A little common courtesy wouldn't do any harm,'' she retorted.

The stationmaster started to speak, looked at her more closely. Some of the hostility faded from his face. ''Folks around here don't care much about being mixed up with the Blaine camp,'' he said, a hint of apology in his voice.

''My aunt doesn't seem to have sent anyone to meet me,'' Julie said desperately. "How can I get there? I know there aren't any taxis. Would one of the village people drive me?"

"Been a storm," the stationmaster said, paying out small coins of information like a miser counting out pennies. "Anyhow, no one would try to get through a drift of snow on that woods road to take someone to Blaine's."

Julie's eyes snapped. "Then they ought to be ashamed of themselves! I thought people in small towns helped each other! That's how we survived in a pioneer country — by helping."

The stationmaster's face softened. There was the beginning of a smile. A thaw was setting in. Then he looked over her shoulder and the ice pack was back.

"Not much helping, up at Blaine's," he said shortly. "Killing's more like it." He slammed down the window again.

"Attagirl," chuckled the man behind Julie and she turned with a start.

He was a burly man, looking even heavier in his thick coat of black-and-white checks, padded cap, high boots. As Julie faced him he reached for his cap and removed it. He had thick hair and big teeth that showed to the gums when he smiled.

There was too much suavity in his voice, too much admiration in his eyes, too much mockery in his smile.

"You are Julie Ames," he said. "My name is Swen Oorth. I like girls with plenty of ginger. In fact, I like girls. Mrs. Blaine asked me to meet you. You'd better come on before the snow gets any deeper. Where's your luggage?"

"Out on the platform in the snow. The stationmaster wouldn't help me. What's wrong with him?"

"Oh, the town people are all like that," Swen Oorth said carelessly. "The whole da — darned bunch. Here, you look half frozen. Mrs. Blaine sent a 'Thermos' of hot coffee. You'd better get working on it while I go after your stuff."

Thankfully, Julie drank the hot coffee; her shivering lessened, she felt comforted and fortified. But her trouble deepened. *The town people are all like that. . . . Killing's more like it.* Something was terribly wrong. It could not be Aunt Deb who was to blame. No one could help being charmed by Aunt Deb. And yet she was surrounded by an aura of hostility. And if the big burly man represented her friends — Julie checked her unruly

31

thoughts. It was unfair to judge him so soon. After all, she remembered, this man had suffered in a Communist prison camp. Some allowances should be made for him.

By the time the "Thermos" was empty, Swen Oorth was back. His bold eyes studied her with open admiration, with the assured insolence of a man who believes his own charms are devastating. Again Julie felt dislike and distrust stir and tried to banish them.

"Okay," he said, "your luggage is all set. Come on." His hand closed around her arm and he led her to the door. Before going out into the cold, Julie looked back. The stationmaster had raised his window again and he was leaning over the counter to watch them, a curious expression on his melancholy face.

As he caught Julie's eye he called, "If you're smart, young lady, you'll go back where you came from." Down went the window.

There was a sleigh outside the station and two heavily blanketed horses, their breath coming in jets of steam. Little bells jingled on the harness as the team stamped their feet.

"A sleigh! Oh, what fun," Julie exclaimed.

Swen Oorth made a sardonic gesture toward the village. "Get what fun you can," he said drily. "The excitement here consists of one movie a week and coffee or ice cream at the drugstore. And the sleigh doesn't mean a joy ride; it means the roads aren't opened yet."

He lifted her effortlessly into the sleigh, held her for a moment unnecessarily close, took her slim ankles and thrust her feet into a fur-lined carriage muff, tucked blankets carefully around her, his bold eyes on her face.

Julie instinctively drew away and he laughed. He got in beside her and took the reins. As the sleigh moved over the frozen snow he turned to her. "You are a stroke of luck. I never dreamed we'd get anything like you up here." He chuckled. "The other — ladies — won't be pleased with the competition."

There had been mockery in his voice as he said "ladies."

Julie glanced at his face from under long lashes. Better not to antagonize him. "I'm glad to know there are other women. It won't be so lonely. What are they like?

Do you know them?"

Swen Oorth laughed aloud. "What I know about the goings-on at the Blaine camp would fill several volumes marked Top Secret. That's quite a place up there. And quite a lot going on. You'd be surprised."

Again Julie fought down her irritation, her dislike of the man's brash manners, his unveiled insolence, his bold assurance.

"That sounds exciting," she said lightly. "What kind of things are going on?"

Oorth chuckled. "I could name a couple of people who would give a lot to know that. But —"

Julie laughed. "So you won't talk!"

"In any case," Oorth told her with a new, harsh note in his voice, "silence is golden. Golden." He added through his set teeth, "It had better be!"

The snow was letting up and the sky was much lighter. Through a break in the clouds sunlight fell in a thin shaft on the frozen snow and blinded the girl with a sudden riot of red, yellow, blue lights that would have dimmed a diamond.

"How beautiful," she murmured. "How beautiful." Her chin was tilted upward, the red velvet cap hugged her face, her cheeks almost matching it in vivid color because of the cold. Oorth looked at her for a long moment.

"Yeah," he said unsteadily, "beautiful."

Ahead Julie could make out dark objects that were the low buildings of the logging camp. Up on the crest of the hill she could see the familiar lines of Jim Blaine's hunting lodge. They had turned into the woods and were following what Julie hoped was a road, though the white expanse was unbroken. The sound of saws rang in the clear, cold air. Vaguely she could hear voices.

"What's that?" she asked.

Oorth told her briefly, "The crews are cutting trees. We're nearly at the camp now, Miss Ames."

Then a man shouted, loud and clear, "Tim-ber-r-r-r."

There was a mighty crack; Julie saw the great tree toppling toward the sleigh. Oorth's lips drew back from his teeth in a grimace of horror. It was an expression of such naked fear as the girl had never seen before. Panic fear.

He tugged at the reins and then, with

a cry, leaped out of the sleigh. Ran from the falling tree.

Julie looked up at it, struggled in a frenzy with the blankets, tried to pull her feet out of the carriage muff in which they were imprisoned. She was so carefully wrapped up that she could not move.

Then strong arms lifted her, tore her free from the blankets. Someone raced frantically, carrying her over the snow. The tree fell with a thundering crash. Snow went up in a cascade. A horse screamed, the harness bells jingling with incongruous gaiety as it lunged and thrashed with terror and pain.

And then there was a silence in the woods. Julie became aware that a man was holding her in his arms, she could feel the thudding of his heart. At length he set her on her feet.

"All right?" he asked.

It wasn't Oorth! She had never heard the voice before and yet it sent a tingle along her nerves.

"I'm all right," she made herself say cheerfully. "Thanks to you." She looked up. Stared into clear eyes under brows that nearly met. The man in the New York restaurant!

"You!" It was a soft gasp that escaped before she could stop herself. Then color flamed into the face that had been white from shock.

He dropped the hands that had steadied her. "Fine," he said coolly. "Before I take you up to the lodge I'd better see how badly the horses were hurt."

"But Mr. Oorth —"

"I'll deal with Oorth later." His voice was quiet but deadly. Suddenly, though she could not like Oorth, though she could feel only contempt for the way he saved himself at her expense, Julie was afraid for him. Oorth would have let her be crushed by the falling tree and she knew that without the last-minute rescue by the man with the gray eyes she would be dead now or horribly crippled. But perhaps Oorth could not help being a coward. She said breathlessly, "He didn't mean to —"

"His carelessness ran you into danger," he said harshly. "His cowardice might have killed you."

"But —"

The gray eyes bored into hers. "So you are another of Oorth's conquests," he exclaimed. "You would defend him even when he turned tail and ran. What a man he must be!''

Julie's face flamed with anger. ''I'm not one of his conquests!'' she denied hotly. ''I thought he was despicable. But no worse than —''

''Than I am?'' He laughed softly. Turned and left her while he went to the sleigh with long strides. It had turned on its side. When Julie saw the wreckage, the splintered wood of the seat, she felt a moment's dizziness. The world tilted. Steadied. She had brushed the very skirts of death.

Again a horse screamed. The gray-eyed man took a gleaming knife from his belt and hacked. What was he doing? Then one of the team struggled to its feet and moved away. He had cut it loose from the harness. The injured horse screamed again and Julie covered her ears to shut out the sound.

There was a crunch of feet on frozen snow. Oorth was coming back. For once there was no trace of his arrogance, his bold assurance. He was sheepish, ashamed. He avoided Julie's eyes.

The other man did not move but there was a revolver in his hand. The gun spat and this time it was Julie who screamed. When she opened her eyes she saw with incredulous relief that Oorth was unhurt. It was the horse that had been shot.

A man came running out of the woods. "What happened?"

Oorth turned on him savagely, glad to have someone on whom he could take out all the anger and shame he felt at himself, someone whom he could make suffer for his own moment of panic.

"Lester," he snarled, "you deliberately planned to fell that tree across the road! That was no accident. You might have killed —"

Lester was as big as Oorth, but solid where the other man was soft. He was a homely fellow with the pale skin of the redhead, a scattering of freckles across his flat nose. At the moment he was chalk-white.

"Not you!" he said contemptuously. "Not at the speed you were running away." He looked at Julie and the laugh died. He looked sick. Then he turned to the dead horse.

"Old Molly," he said and it was almost a sob. "Old Molly. Oh, God, I'm so sorry."

"Have the mare taken off the road, Lester," the gray-eyed man said crisply. "We'll talk about that tree later. All right, Oorth, get back to your crew. I'll take Miss Ames up to the lodge myself."

"Little Napoleon," drawled Oorth. He showed his gums as he smiled but there was no humor in the smile. "Well, I guess the only way you'd get a girl would be by hi-jacking her and pulling rank. It won't do you any good, though. I saw her first."

The hand on Julie's arm tightened until she nearly cried out with pain. Then it relaxed. "Ready, Miss Ames?" the gray-eyed man asked evenly. "Your aunt has some hot breakfast waiting for you. Welcome to our wilderness, the place where anything can happen!"

III

As Don Bruce flung open the front door of the Blaine hunting lodge, which temporarily had been turned into a kind of inn for the married superintendents and their wives, a brown setter rushed at him with a joyous bark and a speed which nearly knocked him off balance.

"Down, Monty!" Don commanded. "Mind your manners. You mustn't frighten our guest. She's had enough fright for one morning." He smiled at Julie and, in spite of her anger for the way he had suggested she had fallen for Oorth, she felt her heart turn over. Never, in her short career as a sensation among the debutantes, with dozens of men on her stag line, had she ever known one who had such an effect on her. Certainly not Quentin Harrington, for whom she had felt a

41

long-standing friendship and affection.

"Fright!" exclaimed a woman's soft voice. "What do you mean? What was that shot, Don? Julie, my dear, welcome!"

Mrs. Deborah Blaine, in purple cardigan and light gray tweed skirt, had been seated at a respectful distance from the flames rushing up the great stone chimney in the room which had once been her living room and now had been transformed into an office. She put down the navy blue sweater she was knitting and came forward with unhurried eagerness to meet her young niece.

Julie studied her face anxiously. Aunt Deb, she thought, was as dainty as a Dresden china figure, like an old French marquise with powdered hair. Behind her fragility there was a strength the girl had never realized before. Without excess formality she had great dignity, mellowed always by a graciousness that was of the heart as well as the manner.

She fitted like a glove in her New York apartment. She had always seemed a little out of place in this rustic hunting lodge. She seemed even more incongruously out of place in this room, whose characteristics had changed — which had become austere, with its big workmanlike desk and filing cases.

"You must be frozen, child! And starved, too. I remembered there was no diner, not even a buffet car, on that train and sent coffee."

"It saved my life," Julie said gaily. "Nothing has ever tasted as good as that did."

"Carrie has breakfast waiting for you." The older woman turned to the man who had accompanied Julie. "You'll join us, won't you?"

"Thank you, Mrs. Blaine. Another time, if I may, I have — things to attend to."

He went out quickly. Things. He meant Swen Oorth! Julie's lips parted to speak and then she changed her mind.

"I thought Swen Oorth was to meet you," Mrs. Blaine said in surprise.

"He did, Aunt Deb, but —"

"Something happened, didn't it, Julie?" the older woman said quietly. Her eyes widened. "That shot! Julie, what was that shot, and why did Don say you'd been frightened enough?"

Julie described the felling of the tree,

the injury to the horse which had been shot, and how she had been dragged out of the sleigh in the nick of time.

The color faded from her aunt's face. Even her lips were white. Remembering the heart condition, Julie was alarmed.

"I shouldn't have told you!"

"Of course you should have told me. Only — these accidents happen too often, Julie. Something is wrong here. Very wrong. And I can't get to the bottom of it."

"Who is the man who brought me up to the house?"

"Don Bruce, my new manager and, like the superintendents, a Korean veteran who was a Communist prisoner. He's a piece of really fantastic luck. A week ago he sent a telegram applying for the position. Came at once — and already things seem to be moving more smoothly. He is wonderful at handling the loggers, and my superintendents liked and respected him at once. And it is a delight to have a man in charge who not only is more than competent but whose manners are invariably charming. He hasn't talked about himself but one can sense cultivation in everything he says and does."

Mrs. Blaine laughed at her own enthu-siasm. "But I'm keeping you from your breakfast while I sing the praises of my manager. I'll show you your room first though you can't change until one of the men brings your luggage from the sleigh."

Holding the railing, walking slowly with frequent rests because of her heart, Mrs. Blaine led the way to the second floor. "The lodge is filled," she said, "so I've had to tuck you into what was the housemaid's room. It has a comfort-able bed and it's warm, but that's about all that can be said for it."

The room was at the back of the house over the kitchen, with a low ceiling, a single bed, dresser, a curtain to cover the long bar with its rows of hangers for clothes, a chair and a small desk. There were bright hangings and a rag rug on the floor. Julie assured her aunt that it would be very comfortable.

As they went down the stairs toward the dining room Julie said, "I haven't seen any servants. You aren't cooking for all these people, are you, Aunt Deb?"

Her aunt laughed. "None of the serv-ants would stay for the winter, but I found a jewel. Carrie is cook and housekeeper. She even makes the beds. I don't know how she finds time for it all, poor soul.''

''What's wrong with her?''

''She has a birthmark on her cheek that's disfiguring and she's pitifully conscious of it. Poor thing. Otherwise she'd be rather pretty.''

''Why,'' Julie asked, ''can't the other women make their own beds? You are doing enough for them by providing a pleasant home and good meals.''

Mrs. Blaine laughed shortly. ''Neither of them has lifted her hand so far. All they do is complain because the wilderness is so dull.''

The wilderness where anything can happen, Don Bruce had said.

Even the dining room had changed, the refectory table was gone and in its place four small tables, each seating two people, were set with flat silver shimmering on the snowy damask. Crimson hangings hung at windows on two sides. Blue-tipped flames, running the gamut of tints and shades of scarlet and green and gold, licked up the stone chimney above which bristled a superb set of antlers.

At one of the small tables orange juice

was waiting. Julie slipped into her place and her aunt sat across from her.

Julie drank her orange juice and studied her aunt. Hair white as snow, silvery snow. Eyes purple-blue as English violets. Lovely skin only faintly lined, nose adorable, mouth with a tendency to curl upward at the corners. Hands patrician, figure slender.

The swing door opened and a woman looked in inquiringly. "All right, Carrie," Mrs. Blaine said. "My poor niece is half starved."

The sturdy woman came in with a tray containing coffee, waffles and sausage. As she set them before Julie she turned her face away self-consciously, trying to conceal the red scar on one cheek.

Impulsively Julie smiled at her. "This is wonderful, Carrie. And thank you for being here. My aunt has been telling me how much it means to her."

The woman's face glowed. "It's nice of you to say so, Miss Ames. I guess you are kind the way your aunt is. It's a pleasure to be helping Mrs. Blaine."

"It's one thing to help and another to be exploited," Julie said crisply. "There are going to be some changes around here.

47

From now on the women can take care of their own rooms.''

''That will be a big help,'' Carrie said fervently. ''If they'll do it.''

''They'll do it,'' Julie assured her and Mrs. Blaine's eyes twinkled.

''Julie, my dear, you are going to be a joy to me. Not only the family beauty but the family balance wheel. No one expects a level head with so much good looks.''

Julie gave a gurgle of laughter. ''A level head. Pig-headed, Quentin thinks.''

Mrs. Blaine's eyes fell on the girl's ringless hand and she looked up, startled. ''Julie! What about Quentin? You haven't quarreled, have you?''

''Violently,'' Julie admitted, a spark glowing in the depths of her eyes. ''He doesn't appear to care for women who have minds of their own.''

''Is it just a lover's quarrel or is it final?''

''I don't know,'' Julie admitted. ''Quentin has always been a part of my life. Perhaps he will be again. But right now, I don't know.''

She poured sirup lavishly on the waffle. ''Is that enough for marriage, Aunt

Deb?''

Her aunt sat with her chin in the palm of one tiny hand. ''Enough, you mean, that you are used to seeing him around?''

''Yes.''

Mrs. Blaine was troubled. ''No one can answer that for another person. It depends on what has the most value for you, what you really want.''

''A happy marriage,'' Julie said promptly. ''A — complete marriage.''

''Then,'' her aunt told her firmly, ''it is not enough.''

''Was yours —'' Julie began. Stopped.

Mrs. Blaine smiled tremulously. ''Yes, it was everything a woman could dream of. That's why I can't bear to have you settle for second best.'' She added meditatively, ''Of course, Quentin is a fine person and reliable. He's wealthy. His social position is like the Rock of Gibraltar. But those things aren't enough, Julie. The money won't make you happy, or society — if it isn't the society of the person you care for most. Even grief and suffering and trouble — real trouble — are worth paying for a good marriage.''

That was why, Julie thought, her aunt accepted so serenely the problems that beset her now. They were a small price to pay for the happiness she had had. And yet she should not be here enduring the rigors of the Maine winter and the strain of worrying about being able to meet her debts and save her husband's estate.

"Aunt Deb," she said impulsively, "are you sure it is safe for you to be here?"

The older woman gave her an amused smile. "You mean because of my heart? Don't worry, my dear. My heart and I have made a pact. It won't fail me so long as I need it. Anyhow —" she leaned forward, her lovely hands loosely clasped.

"I don't know how much Newton Brewster explained to you," she went on. "Jim — my darling Jim — no woman was ever happier, ever more deeply in love or more deeply loved than I, Julie — but my beloved husband had no money sense and he was blindly trusting. I learned a few months ago that he had backed notes for worthless friends. The debts are staggering. But," and her voice was cheerful, incisive, "if we can get the timber cut by the end of March we'll come through, debts paid and everything under control. So we're going to do it."

"But must you stay yourself?"

"I need good men to run the lumber camp, Julie, but they won't stay without their wives, and their wives won't stay without their comforts. It seemed unfair to expect them to do what I was unwilling to do myself, so I've turned my house into a kind of inn, as you can see, to keep the women satisfied."

"It doesn't seem fair, when you are doing so much for their husbands."

"Fair! Don't forget, Julie," her aunt said quietly, "what those men have done for us. They were all Communist prisoners for months. If they want their wives with them now, it *is* fair. Anyhow, now that I have a new manager, things may work out better. How do you like him?"

"Why —" Julie began and found that she could not go on. How did she like Don Bruce? She didn't know. At one moment the sound of his voice sent a thrill through her; the next, she was furiously angry with him. Her attitude toward him was anything but indifferent.

"If anything should happen to him," Mrs. Blaine said, "I would really give up in despair."

"Why should anything happen to

him?'' Julie asked, startled.

''My last manager was killed in a hunting accident. Downing was a fine fellow, very popular in the village, where he had lived all his life. While he lived, everything went smoothly but since his death everything seems to have gone wrong.''

''What is causing the trouble? Haven't you any suspicion?''

''Suspicion, yes,'' Mrs. Blaine admitted. ''Proof — no. Just intuition, I guess. I don't trust Swen Oorth. I think he is a troublemaker. And I don't understand why he is working here. He seems to be much better off financially than the other men. He always has money which he spends lavishly. So why did he come?'' She pressed her finger tips against her forehead and her rings winked in the light from the fireplace. ''Or perhaps I'm just prejudiced. Heaven knows, the other women seem to find him irresistible.''

''Ugh!'' Julie said. ''What big teeth you have. The better to eat you with, my dear! He's a wolf in wolf's clothing. Anyhow, if he were Prince Charming himself I'd never forget that he ran to save his own life, leaving me all tangled up in blankets and that carriage muff. If it hadn't been for Don Bruce —'' she shivered.

Her aunt looked up, smiling. "Come in, Hugh!"

A well-built young man with curly auburn hair and a good-looking face with a cleft chin was standing rather shyly in the doorway.

"Thanks, I've got to get back to work, Mrs. Blaine. I just wanted to tell you I've brought up the luggage from the sleigh. Gosh, that was really a smash, wasn't it! The sleigh was reduced to kindling. But fortunately the suitcases were tumbled out in the snow as it turned over and they don't seem to be injured. Where shall I put them?"

"In the little room over the kitchen. Julie, my dear, this is one of our superintendents, Hugh Gordon. My niece, Julie Ames."

His face lighted up when he saw her. He took her outstretched hand. "Golly, I didn't expect anything like you. I hope you're going to stay a long time."

Mrs. Blaine laughed. "As long as we can make her happy."

"I'm putting in my bid early," he declared. "We'll keep you happy or die in

53

the attempt.''

''You won't need to do anything so drastic,'' Julie assured him gaily. ''I've always loved it up here.''

He waved his hand and went out in the hall. They heard the bags bumping against the railing as he carried them up to Julie's room.

''That's a nice boy,'' Mrs. Blaine commented. ''I'm glad he'll have you to play around with. He's been lonely and I think he's had an unhappy life.''

Julie smiled affectionately. ''People always tell you all their troubles, don't they, Aunt Deb?''

''Hugh has talked to me a bit. He looks on me as a kind of substitute for his mother, whom he adored.''

ii

After breakfast Julie went up to her small room to change. The suitcases were a bit battered and dented but otherwise they had survived the wreck surprisingly well. She unpacked dresses and hung them behind the chintz curtain, filled the bureau drawers, set out toilet articles. While she changed from her traveling suit to a powder blue sweater and suit she thought how altered the Blaine hunting lodge was — how different Aunt Deb's life from what it had been. She still looked fragile and helpless and yet she was carrying through her plan in spite of all obstacles. How she must have loved her husband!

I've never loved Quentin like that, Julie thought. Perhaps Aunt Deb is right and what we feel for each other is not enough for the kind of marriage I want. But it will be hard to convince Quentin.

She ran a comb through the soft dark waves of her hair and went downstairs. Deborah Blaine was sitting at the big desk in the new "office," talking to Don Bruce.

"You've been on the job for a week," she said. "Time enough to know the men and to give you some conception of the work to be done. Do you think we'll finish the cutting by the first of April?"

"We'll finish it," he said quietly.

"Are the men being difficult?"

"On the whole they are good men," Don replied slowly. "Right now they aren't doing their best work. In fact, they work as little as possible unless they are closely supervised. Someone has been upsetting them; they are discontented and hostile. If it weren't for the fact that they probably could not get other jobs for the winter months I doubt if they would stay at all.''

''My former manager, Downing, always said they were as fine a crew of men as he had ever worked with. Everything was going splendidly until his death.''

Don stood at ease, looking down at her, his bronzed face intent. Julie understood how her aunt felt about this man. There was an air of controlled power about him that the girl had never encountered before.

''Just what happened to Downing, Mrs. Blaine?'' Don asked.

Neither of them paid any attention to Julie who settled herself quietly in a chair by the roaring fire.

''He was deer hunting,'' Mrs. Blaine explained. ''A number of hunters were out at the time. He was shot through the head with a rifle. Some careless hunter — probably. No one was ever found who would admit to firing the shot.''

Julie looked up and saw that Don was watching her aunt intently. ''What is it?'' he asked gently. ''Something is worrying you terribly, Mrs. Blaine. That's what I am here for, you know; to take the worry off your shoulders. And the responsibility.''

When Aunt Deb smiled she looked almost young. ''Responsibility,'' she said. ''There are so few people who will accept it — let alone welcome it. I'm very grateful to have you here.''

''But you don't trust me enough to share your burden with me. Is that it?''

Mrs. Blaine's hands played with the pencils on the desk. Then she brought them together with a soft, decisive sound.

''Yes, I trust you. I must trust someone. What — frightens me — is that the day Downing was killed, a hunting rifle was missing from the gunroom — what is now the gameroom. All my husband's rifles and shotguns were in racks on the wall. That particular rifle has never been returned.''

''So,'' Don's eyes were intent, ''you are afraid your manager was killed by the missing rifle.''

''Sometimes, I've — wondered.''

''In that case, it can't be regarded as an accident, can it?''

''But otherwise,'' she said, her breath

coming unevenly, "it would be murder."

"It would be murder," Don said steadily. "And in a way that would explain a lot. It would explain the hostility of the loggers. It would explain the distrust of the village people, who had watched Downing grow up from the time he was a small boy and liked him immensely. It would explain the way people feel about the camp here."

"Murder," Mrs. Blaine said unbelievingly. "I suppose I've always realized the possibility, but I kept pushing it into the back of my mind. I couldn't accept it."

"Do you know anything — anything, Mrs. Blaine, that would account for Downing's murder? Did he seem to have any particular enemy?"

"I remember, the day before the — accident, he told me there was trouble brewing. When I asked about it he said not to worry. He'd be able to handle it himself."

"And he didn't have a chance," Don said. He walked from the desk to the window. Back again, deep in thought. "He was right, Mrs. Blaine. There is trouble brewing. More than one kind. But, at least, the labor end I can deal with. The men are deliberately being stirred up by someone; they won't work unless they are watched all the time. Your superintendents are doing the best they can but we've got to find out where the source of the trouble lies and stop it.''

''Do you think you can do that?''

''I know I can,'' Don said quietly, and again Julie sensed something deadly in his voice.

''You said you could handle the labor troubles. But there's something else, isn't there?'' Mrs. Blaine insisted.

Don hesitated. ''The other thing is women,'' he said frankly. ''There's no place for women here. They are in the way. Everything would move more smoothly if you would all leave.''

''I can't leave,'' Mrs. Blaine said firmly.

''Well, at least send Mrs. Keane and Mrs. Wheeler and Miss Ames away.''

''Tell him I'm not going, Aunt Deb,'' Julie protested. ''I promised to see you through and I intend to keep that promise.''

Deborah Blaine raised her eyes to Don. ''You don't think Julie will be in danger, do you?''

Don glanced at Julie and away again. "She won't be," he said coolly, "but I think she'll prove to be a disturbing influence if she stays."

Julie leaped to her feet, a spark of anger smoldering in her eyes. "Of all the outrageous —"

Her aunt laughed. "We'll let Julie stay," she decided. "On good behavior, at any rate."

"You're the boss, Mrs. Blaine. I hope you won't regret it." He turned without a backward look and went out.

IV

DEBORAH BLAINE turned to face her niece. "I hope," she said soberly, "I'm not making a mistake about this. In some ways, Don is right. Take Curtis Wheeler's bag of tricks, Clarisse —"

"What about Clarisse Wheeler?" The woman who strolled into the office seemed ludicrously out of place in the wilderness, a kittenish blonde moving in an aura of perfume. A tight-fitting knitted dress of pale pink wool outlined a luscious if rather plump figure. At first sight she might be twenty. At second, she was closer to thirty. She had a high sweet voice that had a tendency to become shrill when she did not watch it.

"This is Mrs. Wheeler," Aunt Deb said quietly. "My niece, Julie Ames."

Clarisse Wheeler's small eyes, with

their long artificial lashes, narrowed as she looked from Julie's shining cap of black hair to her beautifully tailored suit. She held out a hand with predatory fingers and long red nails like talons. It glittered with rings.

"Welcome to No Man's Land," she said. "Staying long?"

Something in her tone said, "I hope not." Julie answered crisply, "Indefinitely. Probably until the timber is cut."

"Well," Clarisse shrugged plump shoulders, "it's your headache. At least, there will be four of us to play bridge while the men are gone all day. It's pretty grim with nothing to do. By the way, Mrs. Blaine, I wish you'd speak to Carrie. It's nearly ten o'clock and she hasn't made my bed yet."

Julie tingled with anger. Aunt Deb had turned her home into an inn to make this woman comfortable, and she was being treated insolently, as though she were nothing but the manager. A hot retort rose to her lips and it required a struggle to repress it.

"Come on," she said cheerfully, "I'll help you make your bed. It will be a nice change from bridge. Carrie has too much to do, even without being chambermaid, so from now on we women can take care of our own rooms.''

Mrs. Blaine bit her lips to repress her amusement while the protesting Clarisse followed Julie upstairs. Julie herself was having difficulty to keep from laughing at the plump blonde's expression of chagrin and helpless indignation.

The Wheeler bedroom looked as though a cyclone had struck it. Julie, remembering the room as it had been in the past, wondered that so much disorder could happen in so short a time. The room had old-fashioned wallpaper, a four-poster bed with a chintz canopy, rag rugs, maple furniture, gay curtains. It was charming. Or rather, it had been charming.

Now the bedding dragged on the floor. Negligees and dresses and shoes were strewn over the furniture as though they had been thrown anywhere. The dressing table was a clutter of bottles, jars, creams and lotions. Over everything there was spilled powder. And the air was saturated with the pungent aura of Clarisse's perfume.

With Julie's energetic help Clarisse reluctantly put the room to rights. The bed was made and the clothes hung in the closet.

"What on earth," Clarisse asked discontentedly, "brought you to this dead-and-alive place?"

"I came to look after my aunt," Julie said quietly. "She is taking a big risk, with her heart condition, staying here so that it will be more pleasant for you and Mrs. Keane."

Clarisse flushed. "Yeah," she said, rather ashamed, "it's nice of her, all right. In a way, that is. Of course, my husband wouldn't stay if I left. Why Curtis likes this kind of job I can't imagine. He says it's fine to be out of doors after being shut up in a prison camp."

"That must have been a horrible experience," Julie said.

"I don't know," Clarisse answered. "He never talks about it."

"And bad for you, too. Worrying about him. Being so alone."

There was veiled amusement in Clarisse's eyes as she looked at Julie. "Well, I'm not so unattractive that I had to be alone," she said. "I had plenty of men to take me out, I can tell you. Curtis wouldn't have expected me to sit and brood. What good would that have done him, anyhow, I'd like to know.''

No, Julie thought indignantly, you wouldn't sit and brood. Even if your husband was in danger. You'd never think of anything but yourself and your own amusements and your own petty vanity.

''Heavens, what energy!'' said a low, amused voice in the doorway. The woman was slim, her slenderness accentuated by the plain black wool dress with its simple white collar, almost nunlike in its effect. Like a Madonna's was the smooth brown hair, parted in the middle and fastened in a coil at the back of her neck. Like a Madonna's the pale oval of her face. But not nunlike were the big brown eyes, the full red lips. Looking into those eyes, Julie thought, was like looking into the heart of a volcano.

''Come in, Flo. This is Julie Ames, Mrs. Blaine's niece. Mrs. Charles Keane.''

Florence Keane looked at Julie thoughtfully and held out her hand, murmuring something pleasant in her low voice.

''From now on,'' Clarisse told her, ''we are to make our own beds and clean up our rooms.''

"That's fair enough," Florence Keane said readily. "Carrie has too much to do and heaven knows the days are long. Anyhow —" there was malice in her voice — "you've probably had to make plenty of beds in your time; no use pretending you don't know how."

"Just because you were born rich —" Clarisse began hotly. Then she laughed and her voice lost its artificial sweetness, became shrill. "At least I wasn't married for my bank account."

The pale oval of Florence Keane's face was deadly white. She started to speak. Broke off. Her eyes fell on Clarisse's cluttered dressing table. Julie followed her fascinated gaze. Florence was looking at an odd-shaped medal lying on a tray among the manicure things. She drew in her breath sharply and looked up. Clarisse met her eyes and she laughed mockingly, with a hint of triumph.

With a murmured excuse, Julie went out of the room, closing the door behind her with a long sigh of relief. Talk about tension! Those two women hated each other and yet they shared some secret.

Trouble brewing. Was this what Don Bruce had meant when he urged Aunt Deb to send the women away? And what was the meaning of the odd-shaped medal that had so startled Florence Keane, that had made Clarisse Wheeler look so triumphant?

Lunch — dinner, country-style, Julie corrected herself — was to be served at twelve-thirty. When she went down to the dining room it seemed to be crowded with people, although there were only the four women and four men. Clarisse's husband, Curtis Wheeler, was handsome, ruddy, swaggering, with a booming laugh.

''Well, look what Santa Claus brought us,'' he said as he shook hands with Julie. ''You cheer these old eyes. Mrs. Blaine, why didn't you tell us she was a beauty?''

Florence's husband, Charles Keane, was tall and lean and rangy, less spectacular than Wheeler, but his firm handshake and his smile of welcome were heart-warming.

While Carrie served, Julie looked from one to another of the small tables. Charlie Keane's warm smile had faded as he sat facing his beautiful wife, speaking with formal courtesy only when it was necessary to say something, devoting himself to his dinner without looking up. Florence toyed with her food and sat watching her husband with smoldering eyes.

The Wheelers were bickering in a low tone. He seemed to be amused at something and she was angry.

At the third table Don Bruce sat with Hugh Gordon, the attractive boy who had brought in her luggage. Now and then she saw Hugh look her way and smile. Don, except for a nodded greeting when he came in, paid no attention to her at all. Apparently, Don Bruce did not like women. Except for her Aunt Deb. He had a smile and a gentle courtesy for her although he ignored the three younger women.

Julie noticed, however, that he was alert for every movement, every word of his three superintendents. Without appearing to do so, he was observing them constantly.

''Where's that great hero, Swen Oorth?'' she asked.

Her aunt shrugged. ''He has his meals served alone. He also lives alone in the little cabin behind the kitchen. He's a very — odd person.'' The frown that any mention of Swen Oorth brought to Mrs. Blaine's face dissolved in a smile. ''It's

good to have you, dear. There's something very — fortifying about one's own
family.''

Looking around the dining room, Julie
told herself that these were all normal,
pleasant people. Why, then, was she conscious only of that ominous phrase: *Trouble brewing?*

ii

One. Two. Three. Faintly over the frosty
air came the strokes from the grandfather
clock, drifting through the cold air. Plenty
of time to take a crack at the hill, Julie
thought. She took a quick glance at herself
in her tangerine ski suit, pulled down the
matching cap and picked up her skis.

The porch was icy cold after the warmth
of the lodge but she breathed in the cold
air eagerly, welcomed the tingle of ice on
her face, and bent over to adjust the skis.
Strange how good it was to escape from
that house with its tensions and its forebodings.

All through dinner she had felt as
though she were holding one end of a
time fuse, waiting for the bomb to go off.

Perhaps I'm getting psychic, she told herself. It seemed to me that I could feel danger in the air, that I could taste it, touch it. But where did it come from? The only open hostility was between Florence Keane and Clarisse Wheeler. Is that why Don Bruce believes the women should go?

What was the meaning of the medal which had so startled Florence Keane? What was the meaning of the estrangement that obviously existed between the pleasant Charlie Keane and his beautiful wife? Why did Don Bruce ignore the women and yet seem to be watching the men all through that interminable meal? He had looked from one man to another, frowning. He had listened when one of them had spoken. Did he distrust them?

The snow had stopped and the sky was clear. The air was so crystal clear that the clop of axes and the rasp of saws from the lumber camp at the bottom of the hill drifted up the mountain. There was a shout, ''Tim-ber-r-r!'' the slow splitting fall of a great tree, and the dull thud as it fell. Julie shuddered and felt sick, remembering that terrible moment only a few hours before when she had waited, helpless, while the great tree loomed nearer, nearer over her, when the branches had nearly crushed her as they had reduced the sleigh to splinters, and injured the screaming horse.

Had Swen Oorth told the truth? Had Lester deliberately planned to have the tree fall across the road? But why? Why?

There was a yellow streak, like moving sunshine, as someone in a bright ski suit zigzagged down the white slope. The temperature had climbed to zero. Julie straightened up. It was a perfect afternoon for skiing. Cold as the Arctic Zone. Air full of champagne bubbles. Towering evergreens on each side of the shining black road, which had been cleared since her arrival, rustled with whispers, snapped like popguns from frost in their branches. A white rabbit scurried into view. For a split second it squatted on its hind quarters, stiffened its long ears, regarded her with bulging eyes, stretched its long body and disappeared into the underbrush.

Julie was an amateur and as she looked at the long smooth slope she wondered how adequate her technique was and how much she remembered of the lessons at Lake Placid the winter before. Quentin had been there to guide her, to tell her what to do. The hill seemed unending.

''Here we go,'' she said aloud shakily and pushed off, kicking up clouds of snow, and bumped and skidded down hill, trying desperately to keep her balance.

Darn those movies, she thought. They make it look so easy. Like flying. People soaring and sweeping and making zigzag turns just by a simple twist of the body.

She plodded halfway up another hill and again made a shaky descent. There must be easier ski runs. Far below the lodge, she found a wide, smooth path that suited her.

She tried it over and over until she was warm from the effort and beginning to tire. Without her observing it, absorbed in her strenuous exercise, the light had slowly begun to change.

She had climbed to the top and was poised when a scream rose to a fiercely high note, dropped to a snore, slithered into a bloodcurdling *his-s-s*. The hideous battle cry of the screech owl. Startled, Julie turned her head, lost her precarious balance and fell headlong, face down in the snow.

She sat up, sputtering, wiping snow from her mouth and nose and eyes. Then she looked around. How far had she come, anyhow? She couldn't see the Blaine lodge. There was no sight of the lumber camp, no indication of where the village might be.

I can't be lost, she thought. I simply can't. That's just silly. She struggled to her feet, listening. Somewhere close by she should hear the roaring sound of the saws. But there was no sound at all. The winter silence was broken only by the crack of frost in pines, spruces and hemlocks, by the furtive sound of movement in the underbrush. A lovely purple dusk stole through the forest.

Dusk! Winter days were terribly short. How long had she been skiing? And where was she? In spite of her determination to keep cool she could feel the stirring of panic. She remembered how, the winter before, Quentin had described the horrible experiences of a college friend who had been lost in the Maine woods.

Again there was the sound of movement in the underbrush. An animal? What kind? Bears? But bears hibernated, didn't they?

And from the underbrush came a whisper. "You're lying!"

"How much is it worth to you to have

me keep still?''

''You blackmailer!''

Julie stood motionless. Who was speaking? Man or woman? The whispers did not reveal sex. But they betrayed hatred and gloating and fear.

''I'm not afraid of words. I want cash — unmarked bills — or I'll tell what I know where it will hurt you worst. And believe me, that will be plenty.''

''How much?''

''Five thousand. By noon tomorrow. That's your deadline. Otherwise —''

''Otherwise . . . ?''

''I'll talk.''

''I'll kill you first.''

Julie heard her own sharp gasp. Her heart stopped beating and then began to pound until she was afraid the whisperers in the underbrush could hear it. Her breath caught raspingly in her throat. *I'll kill you first*. Suppose the maker of that threat realized she had overheard those words? She had to get away unseen.

She grasped her poles and then, before she could balance, something struck her between the shoulders and she started a breathtaking descent to the valley bottom. Lost her balance. Skidded. Rolled. And all the time she was thinking, as she plummeted downward, helplessly, ''Someone pushed me! Someone tried to kill me!''

''Hey! Watch out!''

Don Bruce was leaping up the hill toward her. Caught her.

''Are you deaf?'' he shouted angrily. ''One more minute and you'd have been plastered on those treads.''

He helped her to her feet. Not a yard away a tractor, dragging two sleds loaded with logs, was propelling its dinosaurian bulk along a narrow road. Julie swayed for a moment and Don put his arm around her to steady her.

Julie looked up at the tall man who seemed to loom over her. A red wool cap was drawn down to his eyebrows, the collar of a hectic red and green plaid Mackinaw was pulled up to his ears. His eyes blazed with anger as a reaction to the choking fear he had experienced when he had seen the girl in the tangerine ski suit hurtling down in the very path of the tractor.

She did not see the fear, the shock, the tenderness in his eyes. She responded to the anger in his voice. ''Do you think I was skiing on my face for the fun of it?''

she retorted furiously.

"Sorry." In his bronzed face his teeth gleamed white as the snow on the tip of a nearby spruce as he smiled. "But you ought to stay off that hill. It's difficult even for people who know how to ski. Here — you can ride home on one of those loads of logs."

"I don't need your help," Julie stormed. "And I can too ski." She jerked away from his supporting arm. Floundered. Toppled over in the snow.

This time he laughed outright as he pulled her to her feet and she realized that, for all his sternness, he was young. "You're an Olympic champion if you say so," he told her, his face sober, his eyes dancing. "But I'm taking you home. Is that clear?"

Julie nodded. Started to speak, to respond to the laughter in his eyes. Remembered the voices. Remembered the push. Had Don Bruce been one of the whisperers? Had he — tried to kill her? It couldn't be. But Newton Brewster had said, "A dangerous man." She wasn't sure.

Silently she let him remove her skis, lift her onto one of the sleds. Seeing her set face, he turned without a backward look, crunched through snow to the tractor and swung himself to the seat beside the red-capped driver.

Clinging to her precarious perch, Julie wondered: Should I have trusted him? Should I have told him about the whisperers? Should I have told him I was pushed down the hill? . . . But I can't be sure. . . . And yet, if *he* pushed me, why would he have tried to save me?

A wave of relief went over her. A feeling that was very like joy. He can be trusted! How stupid of me not to have thought of that. I'll explain how I happened to fall. I'll tell him everything. . . . Her heart lifted and she sang as the sled swayed behind the tractor.

It was getting very dark. The tractor moved slowly up the hill toward the mammoth log cabin on top, the Blaine hunting lodge that was now an inn. Silhouetted against the western sky it seemed remote and lonely, a reminder of other log cabins, equally lonely and remote, where men had built a crude shelter while they learned to tame a wilderness and build a new land.

The tractor stopped. Don dropped off the seat and came back to the sled. He raised his arms and lifted Julie to the ground. As she was about to speak he said harshly, ''Go back to New York, Julie! This is the second time in eight hours you've barely escaped death. You may not be so lucky a third time. Go back tomorrow. Take the noon train.''

Why was he trying to drive her away? Noon tomorrow! That was the deadline of the whisperer.

''I'm not going,'' she said fiercely. ''I won't be threatened or — or terrorized —''

''Stop talking like a B movie,'' Don snapped, ''I wasn't terrorizing you. But if you know what's good for you —''

''Thanks, Mr. Bruce. I'm the best judge of that.''

He looked down at her. ''I hope so,'' he said gravely and left her.

V

JULIE stumbled up on the porch. Her eyes traveled down the forest-bordered road to the low brown buildings of the lumber camp, snuggled at the base of the mountain, went past to the village where little purple plumes of smoke rose from the house chimneys. Lights were beginning to appear in the mill windows beyond the pond, crimsoned now by the setting sun which tipped the spire of the white church with flame. Through the clear air came the distant barking of a dog and from the hallway the solemn stroke of the tall clock. One. Two. Three. Four. The mountains sent back a spooky echo.

One hour. In that time she had skied and been lost, heard a threat of murder, been nearly killed, rescued, warned away from the Blaine lodge. One hour!

Aunt Deb would know what to do. She would put the whole matter in the older woman's hands. Julie pushed open the door. The office was empty and the fire smoldered in the grate. She went on to the gameroom which, in the past, had been Uncle Jim's gunroom. It, too, had sacrificed its character, to provide amusement for the wives of the superintendents. There was a radio-phonograph, a stack of records, a card table, a ping-pong table, a jigsaw puzzle half finished, a case filled with books, piles of new magazines. All that remained from the past was the rack of guns with their polished stocks.

Deborah Blaine was sitting near the fire, head back, eyes closed. How frail she looked! How worn and anxious she appeared when she dropped the brave mask she wore for the world. Julie's heart sank. You can't tell her. With that heart condition it might kill her. She isn't strong enough for the shock. Her spirit could take it but not her poor tired heart.

For the first time Julie felt truly alone. Alone with a responsibility whose weight she must bear on her own shoulders, a responsibility she could not shift to anyone else, that she could not even share.

As she closed the door behind her, her aunt looked up. The mask was on once more, smiling, cheerful. Something about the older woman's gallantry brought a lump to Julie's throat, a mist to her eyes.

"I'm so glad you're back! I was getting worried. I thought you'd get lost. It's awfully easy to get lost in these woods, Julie. I thought I'd have to round up the logging crew and set them to beating the woods. I don't like to be fussy but promise me one thing. After this, always take Monty with you. A dog is a trusty guide. I'd feel safer knowing he was with you."

"I promise," Julie said huskily. She bent over to kiss her aunt's soft cheek.

"Heavens, how cold you are! Take a long hot bath and rest until supper. Tea first? I've had mine. Serve yourself."

Julie pulled off her heavy gloves and her tangerine wool cap, unzipped her skiing jacket, filled a cup from the silver pot, diluted the brew with water from the copper kettle that was sending up a tiny column of white steam to the accompanying rattle of the cover, laid a couple of sandwiches on a plate and settled among the brown cushions of a broad couch. She bit hungrily into the white bread.

"Fresh mushrooms! You do yourself well in the wilderness, Aunt Deb."

"I wanted the place attractive enough to keep the superintendents' wives contented. But —"

Julie glanced at the tray. "Only two cups. Don't the other women join you for tea?"

"They prefer cocktails! This afternoon they seem to be out somewhere. I thought they might have joined you."

Julie shook her head. "I haven't seen either of them since lunch — dinner. Oh, I did see a streak of yellow skimming down the hill."

"That must have been Florence Keane. She has a yellow ski suit." Mrs. Blaine asked, "What do you think of them, Julie? I've always regarded you as a sound judge of character. Those clear, direct eyes of yours aren't often fooled by pretensions."

Julie hesitated, sipped her tea. "They seem to dislike each other."

Her aunt laughed shortly. "I suppose the joke is on me. I thought they would keep their husbands happy, contented. Instead, they barely stop short of public squabbling."

"Don't worry about it," Julie said gently. "It isn't this place that is to blame, Aunt Deb. Women like Clarisse Wheeler would be discontented anywhere. And Florence Keane — I don't know. I think I've never seen such stormy eyes in so quiet a face. She seems to adore her husband but — I could see at dinner that he was — sort of remote. Perhaps it's the aftermath of war. Have the men said much about their experiences in the Communist prison?"

Her aunt shook her head. "They would prefer not to talk about it. I suspect it was — what is their word? — rugged."

Julie smiled at her aunt. "If they won't tell you about it, they won't tell anyone. People always end by confiding in you."

"Not these men," her aunt admitted. "I've tried to show that I was really interested, sympathetic. Curtis Wheeler just makes a joke and changes the subject. Charlie Keane freezes up. Swen Oorth shrugs his shoulders. The only one who has been willing to discuss himself with me is young Hugh Gordon. But not about his war experiences. Now and then he talks to me about his childhood. He was an only son and his mother was widowed while he was a small boy. I think she had a pretty difficult time educating him by herself. Because he is younger than the other men, he has been pretty much alone here. He has steered clear of the women, which was very wise of him. Lately, he has been spending his time with the loggers, helping some of them improve their education in the evenings, encouraging them to take correspondence courses.''

She broke off to say, ''You look exhausted, Julie. After that'' — her lips trembled — ''that near accident this morning, and all that strenuous exercise this afternoon, you'd better go up to your room and get some rest before supper.''

Julie nodded, picked up her cap and gloves, and went toward the door. If her aunt knew how close she had come to death for a second time that day she would send her back to New York. *You may not be so lucky a third time.*

She was stopped by a half-muffled cry. She whirled around. Her aunt was staring at the wall as though she had seen a ghost.

''Aunt Deb!'' Julie ran to her side, took her cold hand. ''What is it? Your heart —''

Mrs. Blaine said huskily, almost in a

whisper. "Look, Julie! Look! The gun rack!"

"What's wrong?"

"Another hunting rifle is missing."

After a search of the house, Julie had to return to the gameroom, meet her aunt's anxious eyes, and shake her head slowly. The hunting rifle was nowhere in the lodge.

Julie took a long, hot bath and then curled up on her bed to sleep. But she lay wide awake, remembering that cruel blow between the shoulders that had sent her hurtling down the snowy hill. Remembering how Don Bruce had caught her in his arms and then stormed angrily at her. Remembering that he had told her to take the noon train for New York and not come back.

At last she gave up the attempt to sleep, dressed quickly, slipping on a cherry-red crepe dress, in an attempt to lift her own spirits with its vivid gaiety. As she brushed her near-black hair till it shone and coaxed it back into soft waves, snow spatted against the window. A rising wind moaned like an uneasy banshee. The girl shivered.

Somewhere a dog howled hideously.

The sound came again, prolonged, blood-curdling, quavering into a wail.

As Julie came out of her room she heard Florence Keane's voice cry out, "Charlie! What was that?"

"Just a dog. Your nerves are a bit out of control, aren't they, Flo?"

"A bit. Sorry I let go."

"Not getting in your regular outdoor sports lately, are you?"

His voice was quiet, but there was a biting quality in it. If any man spoke to me like that I'd never forgive him, Julie decided. And if I loved him, it would break my heart.

Florence Keane gasped. "Charlie!" she cried. "What's wrong with us, darling?"

"What's right with us, Flo?" the man replied dully.

Julie, her ears burning, fled past the closed door of the Keanes' bedroom beyond which the voices had come. The Wheeler door stood wide open. The room was empty. It looked as disorderly as though Julie and Clarisse had never put it to rights. As usual it reeked of heavy perfume.

Clarisse Wheeler was the only one in

the gameroom when Julie went in. Again she was in pink, this time low cut, leaving her shoulders bare. Julie grinned to herself. Clarisse was half frozen. She must care a lot about the appearance she made to pay such a price for it. She was turning the radio dial as Julie went in. Quickly her eyes summed up the girl, saw that the cherry-red dress killed her pale pink one, and scowled.

She snapped off the radio. "Blizzard due tonight. Coming down from Canada. That's all we needed to make things just ducky."

In a moment Florence Keane entered the room alone. Again she was in black. Again her hair was smoothly parted and satin smooth, but tonight the full mouth was vivid with lipstick. Her expensive simplicity made Clarisse's finery look like a tinseled Christmas card, Julie thought.

Clarisse, who had no capacity for keeping still, moved restlessly around the room, flicked the pages of a magazine, rearranged a plant on the table, moved a lamp shade. Flo sat quietly in a high-backed chair with something regal in her posture. Her face was serene. Only her eyes smoldered.

Mrs. Blaine came in, wearing a long dress of white wool. She looked disturbed. "It's just as well the men are late tonight," she commented. "I'm afraid supper will be delayed. I just found Carrie in tears. She won't tell me what's wrong. Anyhow, it will probably be another half hour before she is ready to serve."

There were footsteps on the porch, voices in the hallway. The men came trooping in. Curtis Wheeler joined Julie at the fireplace. His face was red from cold and he was in a jovial mood. "Tonight," he declared, "we're going to make whoopee to celebrate your arrival here." He made a sweeping bow. "May I have the honor of the first dance?"

Julie laughed as she dropped him a curtsey. "We thank you, kind sir."

Charlie Keane wandered over to the card table and laid out a hand of solitaire. His wife half rose to go to him and then settled back in her chair, her hands closing hard over the wooden arms.

Don Bruce's gray eyes had searched for Julie the moment he entered the room. He started to go toward her and she turned impulsively to Wheeler and began an animated conversation. Wheeler's booming laugh filled the room. Don, with a shrug, turned away and went to the bookshelves.

Clarisse drifted after him, slipped her hand under his arm. "Where are the others?" she asked. "Where are Swen and Hugh?"

"Not in yet. Their crews were farther away from the house today." Don reached casually for a book on a high shelf, drawing his arm away from those clinging fingers.

Clarisse tapped her foot, jingled her bracelets and then crossed the room and drew up a chair across from Charlie Keane. "Let's make it double solitaire, Charlie," she said.

"Fine." He scooped up the cards and began to shuffle.

Julie saw that Florence was watching the plump woman with the blond curls and that her full red lips were pressed hard together. Clarisse was certainly true to character, the sort of woman who would try to attract every man she could reach. She hadn't got far with Don Bruce.

The front door opened, banged shut. There were running footsteps and Hugh Gordon came in. One look at his face and

Don Bruce had crossed the room in long strides.

"What is it, Gordon?"

The younger man swallowed. "It's Swen Oorth," he said, trying to steady his voice.

"Hurt? An accident?"

"He's been shot through the head."

ii

There was a moment of stricken silence and then, without a word or a sound, Florence Keane toppled out of her chair onto the floor in a dead faint. The card table fell on its side and cards scattered as Charlie Keane leaped from his chair and ran toward his unconscious wife. At the same moment Clarisse Wheeler began to laugh, a laugh that rose to a scream, turned to loud, uncontrolled sobs.

Curtis Wheeler strode across the room, took his hysterical wife's shoulders in his big powerful hands. Shook her until the blond curls bobbed up and down. The alternate laughter and tears went on. He lifted his right hand and deliberately struck her hard across the face. The sound of the slap was like a gun report in the room. The laughter and sobbing strangled in Clarisse's throat. Slowly the mark of Curtis's fingers began to show on her cheek.

"You — you —" she sputtered.

His hands still gripped her. "Take a long breath," he said, his eyes steady on his wife's face. "That's right. Now another. Don't try to talk." His hands tightened cruelly. *"Don't try to talk, I said."* The words came from between his clenched teeth.

Clarisse fell silent, staring back at her husband's cold, watchful eyes.

Swen Oorth — shot through the head! Julie clutched at the back of the chair while the room whirled dizzily. Cleared. Steadied. *I'll kill you first!* So Swen Oorth had been one of the whisperers. Could she have prevented the murder if she had told Don Bruce about the conversation she had overheard? The thought tortured her. And then, clear, deadly, she heard Don's words, *I'll deal with Oorth later.*

Oh, no, no, it can't be Don. It can't. He wouldn't kill a man. But — suppose he did — what must I do now?

Her attention was called from her own

appalling problem by her aunt. Mrs. Blaine had dropped back in her chair, a thin blue line around her colorless lips, her eyes on the empty space in the gun rack.

"Aunt Deb!" Julie dropped to her knees beside her aunt's chair. Mrs. Blaine's lids fluttered open, she made a groping gesture with her hand. Following that unspoken direction, Julie reached in the knitting bag, pulled out a small bottle of medicine. Her aunt lifted three fingers. Julie measured three drops into a glass, added water, held the glass to those paper-white lips.

On his knees, Charlie Keane was trying to lift his unconscious wife.

"Don't do that," Julie told him. "Leave her where she is. A pillow under her feet. No, not her head — her feet. That's right." She ran upstairs and came back with a bottle of aromatic spirits of ammonia, but it wasn't necessary. Florence Keane was coming around. She looked up, saw her husband's set face and smiled tremulously. He picked her up in his arms.

"I'll take her to our room and see that she goes to bed," he said quietly.

Florence moved her hand so that it touched his cheek and he jerked back his head as though he had been burned. The hand dropped. Silently he carried her out of the room.

Only then did Don Bruce turn to the ashen Hugh Gordon. "Now, tell me what happened? Where is Oorth? And are you positive he's dead?"

"I saw enough dead men in Korea," Hugh said huskily. "Anyhow, the bullet tore a hole —"

"Where is he?"

"In his cabin. I was coming up from the camp when I heard a dog howl. It was hair-raising. I stopped. Listened. Another howl. I thought the animal might be caught in a trap and then I realized he was near the house somewhere. He was in back, near Oorth's cabin. The door was wide open. Oorth lay on the floor. Shot through the head. Stone dead. The pockets of his leather jacket, of the coat under it, of his trousers, had been pulled out. They were empty. Monty followed me in and crouched on his haunches beside the — the body."

Bending over her aunt, Julie thought: It must have been Monty's howl that turned my blood to ice just before I left the room.

"Any tracks outside the cabin, except yours?" Don asked.

Hugh shook his auburn head. "It has begun to snow heavily and the wind is rising. Nearly blew me off my feet getting up the hill. That would cover any tracks in a matter of seconds."

Don nodded and went to the telephone. Called the State Police. Reported the murder. Then he listened for a long time, the frown deepening on his face.

"Okay," he said at length. "But make it as soon as you can. . . . Yes, I understand the situation. I know you will."

He put down the telephone. "The State Police can't get here before morning. The blizzard has tied up traffic. There was a bad accident from a skidding car along the road, and all the men are busy. I'm in charge here until they come."

He turned to Mrs. Blaine, reached for her wrist, counted her pulse. "Try not to worry," he told her gently. "I'll be back to report as soon as I can. Gordon," his voice was harder, crisper, "get that big kerosene lantern and come with me."

Deborah Blaine's pale lips moved.

"Two men murdered. Please take care of yourself, Don."

He smiled grimly. "I'll be careful." He glanced at Gordon and the two men went out of the room.

After a short hesitation Wheeler followed the other men outside. Clarisse began to whimper. "Murder? It can't be murder. There can't be a killer here in the woods. I'm afraid. I want to go home. Curtis has to take me home tomorrow." Her voice rose to a wail.

"Stop it!" Deborah Blaine's pact with her heart still held. Her eyes were tormented, but the color was coming back to her face; she had regained her composure. "Stop it, Clarisse! You've got to pull yourself together. Make yourself useful for once in your life and see whether you can help Florence."

"Help Flo! Why should I help her? She —" Clarisse checked herself. Her vacuous face hardened. "She is certainly taking Swen Oorth's death hard, isn't she? That faint was a dead giveaway. So that's how —" Again she checked herself. "And Charlie — he came in late tonight."

"Don't be infamous!" Mrs. Blaine sat erect in her chair, her eyes flashing, her

95

manner commanding. "A murder charge is the most terrible one anyone can bring, Clarisse. And for the record, Charlie Keane was the only man in the house when Monty howled. All the others were late tonight."

"But it couldn't," Julie began in horror, "it couldn't have been — one of them."

And then her eyes followed the anguished eyes of her aunt, which were fixed on the empty space that had held a hunting rifle.

After that, no one spoke. The three women waited for what seemed hours, with only the loud ticking of the hall clock to break the tension indoors. Outside the storm drew nearer, intensified. The wind rose, snow beat on the window-panes. Julie, crouching near the big fire, shivered as she thought of the man lying dead in the cabin. Only that morning he had met her at the station, vitally alive, self-confident. "So you won't talk," she had said laughing. "In my case silence is golden," he had replied. He had asked for the price of his silence and been paid off in death.

There were light footsteps on the stairs and the three women stiffened, alert, frightened. For the first time they realized clearly that murder had been done, that murder meant a killer, that the killer was somewhere close at hand. And they did not know his identity!

Then Florence Keane came in, wearing a Copenhagen-blue wool robe. Again Julie was struck by the contrast between the quiet face and the unquiet eyes.

"Shouldn't you be in bed?" Mrs. Blaine asked her, concerned by the white face, the shadowed eyes.

Florence made a desperate gesture. "I couldn't stand being alone. I had to know what is happening."

"I thought your husband was with you," Mrs. Blaine said in surprise.

"No, he went out to help the other men."

Clarisse jumped to her feet. "Someone's coming!"

VI

THE BIG LANTERN that Hugh Gordon was holding revealed white swirling snow through which it was impossible to see anything. The wind struck Don Bruce like a heavy wall and he staggered back from its force, blinded by the snow. No wonder young Gordon had seen no footprints outside Oorth's cabin. They were filled as fast as they were made.

For a moment Don took his bearings, his eyes on the light still pouring from Oorth's cabin. He started forward, staggered, skidded. He linked Gordon's arm with his and, head down, the two men battled the ferocity of the blizzard, fighting their way the few yards to the cabin.

Don turned the knob and they lurched in. It required their combined strength to push the door shut behind them and even in that brief interval snow sifted over the floor, over the rag rugs.

Don leaned back against the closed door, panting, and looked around. As Gordon started forward he said sharply, "Wait! Stay where you are! I don't want anything disturbed until the State Police get here."

Hugh gazed at him, surprised by the unaccustomed tone of authority.

"Tell me," Don went on, "just what you did when you came in here. Where you went. What you touched."

Hugh answered promptly. "I stayed right here. I could see at a glance that Oorth was dead. I just took a long look and then beat it."

"You didn't touch anything?"

Hugh shook his head.

Behind them there was a loud, "Hey!" A heavy fist banged on the door. Don turned to admit Curtis Wheeler, who shook snow off his shoulders like a big burly dog and looked around curiously, his high color fading.

Swen Oorth's cabin was a one-room affair with a couch-bed, several easy chairs, a couple of tables and lamps, a desk and a radio-phonograph. The lamps were lighted. There was a highball glass half filled on a table beside an easy chair drawn up to the fireplace. Only one glass, Don noticed. A man's voice was singing, "Home on the range," and the living voice made prickles go down Don's spine until he realized that a record was playing on a record changer. Heaven knew how long it had been on. No way of judging time by that.

The room was neat and orderly, the floor waxed. Nothing had been disturbed. Swen Oorth lay on his face on the floor in front of the fireplace. Evidently the bullet had gone in through the forehead for a great hole had been torn in the back of his head.

Someone was calling and Don turned to admit Charlie Keane.

He took a swift look around, his eyes widening as he stared at Oorth's quiet body. "I just came to see whether I could help."

"There's nothing anyone can do here," Don told him, "until the State Police arrive in the morning. I'll lock up the cabin and —"

Behind him someone moved. He turned swiftly, aware of that furtive movement, but all three men were standing still when he looked at them. He started to speak, checked himself, and finally stood back.

"All right. Sorry to keep you out on a night like this, but you men will have to check on your crews, find out where they spent the past hour and whether they are all present and accounted for. Though I'm pretty sure no one will be missing. To kill Oorth and then run for it would be tantamount to putting a halter around their own necks."

He took the key out of the lock and waited for the three men to pass him. As they did so his eyes rested searchingly on each one, trying to fit the man with an old memory that was becoming blurred, like a negative exposed to the light.

He staggered across the intervening space to the lodge's kitchen door and turned for a last look back at the cabin, with a feeling of sick failure such as he had never before experienced. This had happened when he was practically on the spot. And he had talked of the Bruce luck!

Something evil was afoot here. Oorth's death, if he were right in his estimate of the situation, was the second murder to take place at the Blaine camp. There was no doubt in his mind that someone at the lodge itself had deliberately shot the former manager. He thought he knew why.

An impulse made him return to the cabin. He went in and moved close to the body lying so quietly in front of the fire; bent over and turned the head gently so that he could see the face. He caught his breath in a surprised gasp. Whatever he had expected, it was not what he found. He looked for a long time, incredulously, and then put the head back where it had been.

Well, he had been wrong all the time. He was on a false trail. He had been looking for one kind of trouble and he had stumbled into another, one which did not concern him. As he knelt beside Oorth, something cut into his knee. He straightened up, felt on the rug, and picked up an odd-shaped medal. He turned it over and over in his fingers.

Then he closed his eyes, trying to see the room as it had been when he and Hugh Gordon first entered it. He brought back the picture, piece by piece, as one would fit together a jigsaw puzzle. Then he took a long breath. He was right! The shining medal had *not* been on the rug when he had first entered the cabin. He had scrutinized every inch of the room that was visible from the door before he had taken a step forward, hunting for footprints on the polished floor.

One of the three men with him had placed the medal there, practically under his eyes. Or tossed it. He had been aware of movement. But why? Why? He put the medal back where he had found it, then on impulse picked it up and put it carefully away in his billfold.

In the lodge kitchen, which was empty, Don stripped off his snowy jacket and pulled off his boots. Where was Carrie and what had happened to supper, he wondered. He'd give a lot for a hot meal.

As he went toward the gameroom he heard Clarisse cry out, "Someone's coming!" He went at once to Mrs. Blaine, who was waiting for him to speak, and said heavily: "It's murder all right. There's no weapon."

Her lips turned paper-white but her eyes were steady and her voice even. He felt a throb of admiration for her.

"But why?" she asked. "Robbery?"

Don remembered bending over the

body, observing that the pockets had been pulled out. ''We are supposed to think so.'' He turned then to Clarisse, who was clinging to his arm. Her eyes were frightened but, instinctively, she pressed close to him. An inveterate flirt. With a feeling of distaste he moved away from her.

Florence Keane, her enormous eyes shadowed, sat huddled by the fire in the long blue robe, which she had pulled tight as though she were chilled. Her eyes were a huge question mark but she did not speak at all. He looked at Julie, a bright spot of color in her cherry-red dress, and felt his somber heart lift at the very sight of her. It dropped again at what he saw in her eyes, a look of doubt. She didn't trust him!

He shook his head, trying to push Julie into the background of his mind. This was no time to confuse the issue by his personal feelings.

''Your face is so grim,'' Mrs. Blaine exclaimed. ''Whatever it is, we can take it, Don.''

''I know that you can take it,'' he said. ''You are a pretty wonderful woman, Mrs. Blaine.'' She smiled at him and he went on quietly, ''Oorth's pockets were all emptied, turned out. But it was rather stupid because nothing else in the room was disturbed. He wouldn't be likely to carry all his money on him, though he did have a foolish habit of broadcasting the fact that he always had a lot of cash on hand.''

''But what is there to buy in this wilderness?'' Mrs. Blaine asked in surprise. ''Most of the men just deposit their checks and don't even cash them for weeks at a time.''

''I think he liked the feeling of having plenty on him to compensate for the years when he had to look twice at a dime before he spent it.''

Don watched Mrs. Blaine. A dainty Dresden figure with steel inside it. She seemed too frail to do anything but she had settled down for the bitter winter to see through the paying of her dead husband's debts. She faced the hideous situation of two men murdered at the lodge and a killer loose. She didn't panic. She tried to study the situation with coolness and intelligence.

Julie stood behind her, one hand on her aunt's chair. She'll be like her aunt as she grows older, Don thought, and again the warmth crept into his heart. Whatever comes, she'll find the strength and the courage to tackle it. And smile while she's doing it.

"But where," Mrs. Blaine said suddenly, "where could Swen Oorth have got so much money? It has always puzzled me. I've never understood why he came here."

"Unless," Don said abruptly, "the source of that money is here."

Mrs. Blaine puzzled over his words. Suddenly her lips quivered. "I think I've been trying to make myself believe the motive was robbery. I've been telling myself that more crimes are committed for financial gain than for anything else, whether it's called love or revenge or jealousy or whatever. But I'm afraid, Don. I wonder how much I am to blame, trying to get the timber cut against odds. My first manager shot. Swen Oorth shot. And the guns that killed them may have come from this room. It's too much of a coincidence that a hunting rifle disappeared from this room each time a man died. I can't escape that fact, that responsibility, any longer. Have I opened Pandora's box and set a lot of evil spirits loose in this wilderness?"

He crossed the room to her in swift strides, reached for her small cold hand, lifted it to his lips. "Believe me, Mrs. Blaine, you have nothing to blame yourself for. Sooner or later, Swen Oorth would have died by violence. It was in the cards."

"One of the crew then? I told you there had been trouble with them ever since Downing died."

"I don't know. I almost hope so. Wheeler and Keane and Gordon are all checking on their men now. I can't help hoping it will prove to be one of them."

"But why, Don? Why?"

"Because otherwise," he said levelly, "it's got to be one of us."

"That's ridiculous," Clarisse said shrilly. "That's libel. You could go to jail just for saying that."

"Oh, no, no!" Florence Keane cried out in anguish. "You can't be right. No one would — hate him so much. It has to be robbery."

Don looked somberly from one woman to the other. "There's something I haven't told you yet. There are long scratches on Oorth's face. Look as though they had been made by a woman's fingernails. If we can check on the whereabouts of all the cutting gang it looks as though we'd have to start hunting for the woman in the case.''

ii

Julie stared in horror and unbelief at Don Bruce as his gray eyes moved from face to face, and the four women looked back at him, blankly. The woman in the case! Did he — could he — mean that a woman had killed Swen Oorth? He must be mad. Seeing those gray eyes, now as frosty as the windowpanes, brush over her face, Julie tingled with rage. How dare he make such an accusation?

''Suppose,'' he suggested, ''we go into the office to continue this conversation. It will make it seem more official. Have you any objection, Mrs. Blaine?''

''Make what seem more official?'' she asked.

''The State Police are held up by the blizzard. Until they get here I am in charge. I'm afraid I'll have to ask some questions, clear the ground as much as I can before they arrive.''

Julie expected an emphatic refusal from her aunt. Instead, the older woman rose promptly to her feet. ''Of course, Don. I'm sure we will all co-operate with you in every way we can. I am only sorry that you have so unpleasant a duty added to your other problems.''

He smiled at her, a smile that held respect, gratitude and unexpected sweetness. Why, Julie wondered, had he never looked at her in that way? He always seemed to be angry when he spoke to her.

Clarisse and Florence had not moved. ''Are you ready?'' Mrs. Blaine asked them.

''I'm not going,'' Clarisse said shrilly. ''He can't make me. Anyhow, Curtis told me not to talk.''

''There's no reason why we can't wait for the officials who have proper authority,'' Florence said, white to the lips. ''I realize that we must answer their questions but I cannot accept Don Bruce's authority in this matter.''

Soft eyes like English violets studied the two women for a moment. Then Mrs. Blaine smiled. ''Don Bruce has the authority,'' she said gently but with firmness in her voice. "Not only because I have given it to him but because the State Police have put him temporarily in command. We owe him all the help we can give him in this painful case. And if we fail to co-operate, I am very much afraid that the State Police will wonder what we are afraid of. Shall we go to the office without any further discussion?"

Their protests silenced, Clarisse and Florence followed her out of the game-room and down the hall to the office. Without appearing to dominate, without raising her voice or issuing commands, she had an instinctive ability to control a situation when she chose to do so. Watching that slender, erect figure, Julie felt a lump in her throat. I hope I'll be like that when I am her age, she thought.

Don followed her down the hall. Julie felt an almost uncontrollable impulse to turn and tell him about the whispered conversation she had overheard. She knew now that one of the whisperers had been Oorth. And then she remembered Don saying, "Take the noon train." Was it coincidence that he had mentioned the same time that Oorth had mentioned? How could she be sure? Had he dealt with

Oorth, as he had threatened to do?

He stood back to let her enter the office. She turned toward him and her lips parted to speak. His eyes blazed down at her and again she felt as though an electric current had run between them. She clenched her hands, trying to fight against the thing that drew her toward this unknown man. Then she brushed past him hastily, without speaking.

Don's lips compressed into a thin line. He let her go. Then he sat at the big desk and took out a pad of paper and a pen. His face was bleak, official. The current was broken between them now.

"We'll start with you, Mrs. Blaine. What I'm trying to determine now is the approximate position of everyone at the time Swen Oorth was shot. Of course, until the doctor can get through to us and examine the body we can't be sure, but it seems likely that Oorth died within the last hour. The fire was still burning in the fireplace; there were a couple of small logs which had just begun to blaze. The phonograph was running. Monty's howl probably indicates the time of the death."

"But why," Julie put in, "would it be possible for us to hear Monty howl and

111

not hear the shot?''

Don looked at her and away again quickly. ''That's a good question. We'd have heard the shot if it had been fired any earlier. Only one thing muffled it — the blizzard and the rising wind. Monty's howl was heard because he kept it up as he ran back and forth from the cabin to the kitchen door. Now, I'd like to go back over the whole afternoon, please.''

Mrs. Blaine frowned as she thought back. Then her face cleared. ''After dinner, I rested in my room for an hour.'' She smiled faintly. ''I have an alibi because Carrie was with me. We were planning a week's menus. Then I came down here to the office, paid some bills and wrote letters. After that, I had tea in the gameroom and read and knitted until it was time to dress for supper. Julie was with me part of the time. I came downstairs a little before six and talked to Carrie in the kitchen. Then I returned to the gameroom and I was there when Hugh Gordon came in to tell you about finding the — finding him.''

Don wrote rapidly. ''Did you hear the dog howl?''

The older woman shivered. "It was horrible. That was while I was in the kitchen with Carrie and I could hear the sound distinctly. Monty was right outside Swen Oorth's cabin then."

Don got up to stir the fire and put on more logs. He knelt close beside Julie, his broad shoulder brushing her skirt. She looked down at his bent head, at the strong competent hands using the fire tongs. Something about his nearness stirred her blood. She wanted to stretch out her hand and touch his hair. She moved back abruptly out of reach. He noticed her withdrawal. He turned to look at her.

"You needn't be afraid," he said under his breath.

Color flamed in her cheeks. How dared he look at her like that? First he accused her of falling for Swen Oorth. Now he seemed to know — that is, she corrected herself quickly, he seemed to think she had fallen for him.

She tried to think of something devastating to say in reply but Don did not wait. He returned to his desk, picked up the pen. Once more his manner was blandly impersonal.

"Mrs. Blaine, do you know anything

that would help the police?'' When she hesitated, he leaned forward. ''I must make this clear to all of you,'' he said slowly and distinctly. ''There is a killer loose. If you know anything, anything at all, it is your duty to speak. Not only your duty, but quite possibly it may be your only safety.''

Your only safety. The words had been quietly spoken but they might as well have been shouted. Instinctively, the four women drew nearer to the fire, as though a primitive memory had reminded them that fire was man's first bulwark against threatening danger. They looked over their shoulders. But this was a danger they did not know how to avoid. It might lurk behind a trusted face.

''I don't know anything that would help,'' Mrs. Blaine said slowly. ''I really don't know anything about Swen Oorth, beyond the fact that, like the rest of you men, he had been a Communist prisoner. I tried to talk to him because I like to maintain personal relations with people I employ, but he had little to say — to me.'' There had been a pause. He had talked to others, then.

She went on with a slight blush. ''I

should be ashamed to say this, now that he is dead. But you want the truth. Frankly, I never liked him, never quite trusted him. Because of his war experiences, I tried to put aside my prejudices."

"Did he ever discuss his war experiences?" Don asked her.

"Not with me, at any rate."

"Or his background? Ever mention where he had worked before?"

She shook her head. "You know, I waived the whole question of references."

Without warning Don turned abruptly. "All right, how about you, Clarisse?"

The plump blonde huddled near the fireplace stiffened as he spoke her name and then she tried to look amused. Don glanced at her and then stripped off his sweater and put it over her bare shoulders. Clarisse relaxed as she pulled the warm wool close around her.

Julie found her own eyes resting in fascination on those long pointed fingernails. Had they left the scratches on Swen Oorth's face? Why had Clarisse gone into hysterics when his body was found? From the beginning, at the very first sight, Julie had known Clarisse was not the kind of woman to lose interest in other men when she married. She had been flirting with Charlie Keane only an hour before; she had tried to flirt with Don.

Clarisse looked up, saw the four pairs of eyes watching her. The small eyes narrowed beneath the preposterous artificial lashes. Under that empty face it was obvious that she was thinking hard, that her wits were alert.

"I tried to go for a walk after dinner but it was too cold."

Did Julie imagine it or did Florence Keane stiffen in her chair, her face tense and alert?

"I came back. Washed out some clothes, shampooed my hair and set it." Her hands went up to pat the blond curls. "Did my nails. Took a nap. Ye gods, what is a girl to do with her time in the Maine woods? Go out and talk to the rabbits and the foxes? Feed the deer? Build a snowman? I don't know what I did. I got through the afternoon somehow without screaming my head off from sheer boredom and that's more than I can do most days. Then I made a cocktail and got dressed for supper."

"How long were you outside?" Don

asked.

"Not more than ten minutes and I nearly froze. I told Curtis I ought to have a new fur coat. I haven't been outside the house since two o'clock. I'm sure of that."

"Did you hear Monty howl?"

For the first time Clarisse appeared uncertain. She hesitated, seeming to weigh pros and cons. Then shrugged her shoulders. "If I heard him it didn't register. He's always yapping."

Don tapped his pen on the table, did not look up. Julie felt her stomach muscles tighten as she waited for him to speak.

"How well did you know Swen Oorth, Clarisse?"

VII

"THAT'S none of your business," she snapped, the high sweet voice acquiring a strident edge.

"Not mine, of course," he agreed readily. "Right now I'm just a stand-in for the police."

"Then let them ask me," she said.

"I will," Don told her coolly.

"And there's one point you overlooked," Clarisse said viciously. "You talked about Swen picking up some money here in the wilderness. Well, where would he get it? There's only one person here who's got stacks of money and that is Florence."

"Clarisse," Mrs. Blaine intervened swiftly before Don could speak, "I cannot tolerate that kind of behavior in this house. You and Florence are both my guests. I must ask you to remember it. Ugly and unsubstantiated accusations are not to be made again. If you can't refrain from them as a matter of good taste, it might be well to recall that they are a legal as well as a social offense.''

Clarisse flounced away and sat on the broad window seat, turning her back to the room.

''Florence?'' Don said, a query in his voice.

Florence Keane turned the pure oval of her face to him. How beautiful she would be, Julie thought, if her expression were not so frozen.

''I went skiing after dinner,'' she said. ''I needed the exercise. I had to get out — it chokes me to be penned up.''

''Not getting in your regular outdoor sports lately,'' Charlie Keane had jeered, and Florence had cried out with pain in her voice, ''Charlie! What's wrong with us, darling?'' Julie remembered his bitter reply, ''What's right with us, Flo?''

''Do you have a yellow ski suit?'' she asked, without thinking.

Don frowned at the unexpected interruption and Florence's lips trembled for a moment. ''Yes,'' she said huskily.

"Then I saw you going down the slope. You're really good." Certainly, Julie thought, puzzled, her comment was harmless enough, but both women were as motionless as though they had been turned to pillars of salt.

"Did you see anyone while you were skiing?" Don asked.

Florence considered. "I took the easy ski run that leads to the logging camp. There were a couple of men there: the camp cook, I think, and someone else." Her brows puckered. "Oh, yes, that big man — Lester. He was burying a dead horse."

"What is it, Florence?" Don asked as she hesitated.

"Lester was raging about Swen; said he was trying to get him into trouble with the boss — with you, Don. Said he'd — get even."

Clarisse was listening intently as though there were something momentous about to happen. Florence ignored her but she could not control the color that surged into her face under the other woman's malicious eyes.

Don wrote down what Florence said. He made no comment. His silence bothered her, drove her into further explanation. "I came back here about three-thirty, got a book from the gameroom and went upstairs to read. Then I dressed for supper."

"Did you hear Monty howl?"

"Yes," she said and suddenly her face came alive. "Yes, I did. And Charlie was with me at the time, so it couldn't have been Charlie." Then, belatedly, she clapped her hand over her mouth.

"No one has accused Charlie," Don reminded her evenly. "No one has been accused yet. Did you know Swen Oorth well?"

"I" — color flooded the pale face — "I skied and skated with him now and then."

"I'll say you did," Clarisse began — looked at Mrs. Blaine, and fell silent.

Florence made no response to her but her hands clasped as she said earnestly, still speaking to Don alone, "Charlie is — too busy to go along, and he didn't mind." She added breathlessly, "He didn't mind at all."

"Julie," Mrs. Blaine interrupted, "I'm worried about Carrie. The men will be coming back at any time and they will be half frozen and terribly hungry. Something must be done about a hot supper for them. Will you see what is happening in the kitchen and what has become of Carrie?''

Julie nodded. ''If she isn't there I'll fix something myself. I might as well turn that course in the Brides' School to some account.''

She pushed open the kitchen door and found a cheery, lamplighted room. Red and white checked gingham hung at the windows and cushioned the chairs. Carrie had returned and she was working at the big stove, making coffee, bowls of hot soup and sandwiches, scrambling eggs and frying bacon.

She turned and Julie was startled. Her eyelids were puffy and inflamed. The red scar on her cheek stood out vividly on the pasty skin. She looked like a woman who had faced an intolerable loss, who had been bereaved of what she most loved.

Julie tried to smile at her but Carrie turned back indifferently to the stove, her sturdy body slumping.

''The men aren't back yet,'' Julie said, ''but Mrs. Blaine was worried about them. They haven't had any supper —''

"I got it half cooked," Carrie said dully, "and then I got a headache. When I came back, they'd all gone out and the whole meal was burned or spoiled. So I'm fixing something quick and easy, but at least it will be hot and it will nourish them."

"Thanks a lot, Carrie," Julie said. "You're really a jewel. How is your head? You look as though it were pretty bad."

The woman's face twitched convulsively. "It *is* pretty bad," she said.

"Oh, there they are!" Julie went hastily into the hallway as the front door banged open with an icy rush of wind and Curtis Wheeler came in, slapping snow from his coat and brushing it away from his eyes, stamping his feet to restore circulation.

Mrs. Blaine had risen from her chair by the fire in the office. They were all on their feet, waiting. Clarisse ran forward and caught her husband's arm.

Carrie was standing in the doorway to the kitchen and Mrs. Blaine said quickly, "Carrie, will you bring some hot coffee at once to Mr. Wheeler?"

Don looked a question and Wheeler shook his head. "Whoever killed Oorth, it wasn't one of my lot. They all alibi each other from three o'clock on this afternoon. And they are all present and accounted for.''

A moment later Charlie Keane appeared. His men, too, were in the clear.

The kitchen door opened and Carrie came in with a heavy tray. Just then Hugh Gordon opened the front door. ''I guess it's all over but the shouting,'' he said soberly. ''One of my gang is missing.''

''Who?'' Don asked sharply.

''Lester. The fellows told me that he and Oorth had a set-to this afternoon.''

There was a crash of china as Carrie let the tray slip from her hands. She gave a savage cry.

''No, it wasn't Lester! He's being framed.''

Don reached for his Mackinaw. ''Sorry — you won't have time for supper,'' he said. ''Guilty or innocent, Lester must be found at once. No one could live through a night like this without shelter.''

The big clock struck twelve times. Midnight. At this time last night, Julie thought, I was in the Pullman on the train from New York. Only one day had passed!

On the other side of the fireplace in the gameroom Aunt Deb kept vigil with her. She had quietly but steadily resisted all Julie's attempts to send her to bed, although both Clarisse and Florence had gone upstairs an hour before.

''I must wait until the men come back safely,'' she said. ''This place is my responsibility, Julie.''

So they waited, staring at the red glow on the hearth. What pictures Aunt Deb saw Julie could not guess. Her own mind seethed with conflicting pictures and disturbing memories. In the cabin behind the lodge Swen Oorth lay dead with a bullet through his head. Somewhere out in the blizzard the big logger, Lester, was hiding in the storm. Had he found a shelter? She hoped so with all her heart. Guilty or innocent, she would not have a man out in that blizzard.

When she had seen him briefly that

morning she had been so shaken by her narrow escape from death that she had paid little attention to him. He had been a big man, she remembered, and he had been shocked when he saw Julie, and knew how close the tree had come to crushing her to death. He had been more shocked, grieved, when he saw the injured horse which Don had had to shoot. There had been a sob in his throat when he cried out, ''Old Molly! Oh, God, I'm so sorry.''

But when Oorth accused him of felling the tree on purpose, there had been his mockery at Oorth's cowardice; there had been contempt and something very like hatred. But they had been direct emotions, she decided. It was easier to imagine Lester knocking Oorth down with his fists than shooting him. The wind screamed in the night and Julie shivered. Lester was not, she remembered, the only man out in that blizzard. Surely the others would return soon. They would not be able to endure that cold much longer. They could so terribly easily get lost in the swirling snow. Meantime, she and Aunt Deb must fill the woman's immemorial role of waiting.

The pine walls of the gameroom glowed softly in the light from the two lamps that were still burning. The room revealed the chaos brought by Hugh Gordon's dramatic entrance, his unbelievable statement. Swen Oorth dead. Shot through the head.

The card table lay on its side, with cards still scattered on the floor where Charlie Keane had spilled them when he had leaped to his feet and gone to his unconscious wife. He had cared, he must care, for his beautiful wife, and yet when she had touched his cheek lightly he had jerked his head away as though he could not endure her touch. Strange.

Was Clarisse right? Had Charlie Keane married Florence for her bank account? Florence was afraid for her husband. That had been obvious when she answered Don's questions. Why had she fainted at the announcement of Oorth's murder? Lines from *Hamlet* came back to her: "What's he to Hecuba or Hecuba to him, that he should weep for her?"

Was Charlie Keane jealous because Oorth had taken his wife skiing? Stop it, I have no right to speculate like this. Lester has run away. Lester is guilty. And he and Swen Oorth hated each other.

But why do I want to believe Lester is guilty? Because I don't want it to be Charlie Keane. Or Curtis Wheeler, for that matter. And yet Curtis Wheeler's hands had bitten cruelly into his wife's shoulders, he had slapped her to check her hysteria, he had repeated, "Don't talk!" . . . *Don't talk?* What had he been afraid that she would say? Clarisse had refused to tell Don how well she knew Swen Oorth. Had her nails made the scratches on his cheek? The reckless come-hither invitation in Swen Oorth's bold eyes when they had first met at the station came back to her. She had found him insolent, but perhaps he was attractive to other women. And yet it seemed impossible that a woman had shot him. What did Don mean by "the woman in the case"? Clarisse? Florence? Carrie, who had been acting so strangely at suppertime? What could be wrong with Carrie?

The clock ticked on, measuring off the slow passing of the minutes, and still the men did not come. Sleet was mixed with the snow that rattled on the windows. The wind howled and roared. Julie's lips moved in silent prayer for the men out in bitter cold and blinding snow.

"Please let them find their way home," she said. On impulse she got up, opened the curtains wide, lighted all the lamps and switched on the outside lights to help them find their way back.

Surely those were voices? Yes, the men were back! The door opened and they trooped in, stiff with cold, covered with snow. But there were only four: Curtis Wheeler, Charlie Keane, Hugh Gordon, and Don Bruce. Lester was not with them.

Charlie, shivering, came close to the fire. "I never saw anything so good as these lighted windows, Mrs. Blaine."

Carrie came in with a tray which, this time, she deposited safely on a table.

"Thanks, Carrie," Mrs. Blaine said. "We'll serve ourselves buffet style."

Carrie nodded, but she waited, her hands twisting in her apron, for news.

Curtis Wheeler helped himself lavishly and sat on the floor at Julie's feet, putting a well-filled plate and a cup and saucer beside him. "This is the life," he said.

Aunt Deb's brows were raised as she looked mutely at Don. He shook his head. "No trace of Lester," he said soberly. "But he has lived in the Maine woods all his life. He's bound to have found shelter somewhere."

"Are you sure?" Her pale lips trembled.

He nodded reassuringly. Carrie turned and went back to the kitchen.

"Perhaps," Mrs. Blaine said, "Lester made his way to the village and someone there took him in."

"I doubt it," Don said grimly. "The village people don't feel particularly co-operative to the camp here."

"Why?"

"I don't know."

Julie spoke quickly. She repeated what the stationmaster had told her.

"Killing's more like it," Don repeated slowly. "That means the village people believe that Downing was murdered and the fact is being covered up for some reason."

Hugh Gordon stumbled to his feet, white and tired. "I'm off to bed," he said.

Wheeler and Keane went next. Don turned to Mrs. Blaine. "Better get some rest. The police will be here at dawn and you'll be subjected to a lot of questioning before this case is cleared up. You'll need all your strength."

She got wearily to her feet. "I'll be all right, but it's high time to be in bed. Heavens, it's nearly half past one. Coming, Julie?"

"Not yet. I'll do the dishes first. Carrie looked awful and I sent her to bed."

"I'll help you," Don offered.

While Julie dropped soapflakes into the dishpan in the big old-fashioned kitchen, Don carried out the dishes, scraped and stacked them. He was silent, preoccupied. Then Julie noticed that his eyes were riveted on her hands. Her heart thudded. Was he looking at her nails? Did he think she made the scratches on Swen Oorth's face?

She looked up and saw a flame glowing in his eyes. "The first time I saw you," he said abruptly, "was in a New York restaurant. You were wearing a green velvet evening dress and you had a big emerald ring on your finger. What happened to it?"

"I gave it back," Julie said. Something in his expression made her face burn as it had done when they had exchanged that first long startled look of recognition. To break the spell she began to talk feverishly.

"Don, there's something I didn't tell

you when you were questioning us.''

He reached for a dish towel and began to polish a glass. ''Yes,'' he said quietly. ''I felt that.''

She told him about the whispered conversation she had overheard on the hillside and the threat, ''I'll kill you first.''

''You didn't know who they were?''

''Not then. I'm sure now that one was Oorth. Probably the other was Lester.''

''Perhaps,'' Don said in an odd voice. ''Why didn't you tell me this sooner, Julie?''

''Would it'' — her voice broke — ''would it have made any difference?''

''You mean — would it have prevented the murder?'' When she nodded, he said, ''I am afraid not. Probably nothing could have saved Oorth in the long run.''

''But what had he done?'' she burst out.

''It wasn't what he had done; it was what he knew. Something so dangerous to someone that he had to be silenced.'' Don began to put the dishes in the cupboard. ''But why didn't you tell me sooner, Julie?''

She looked up at the steady eyes, the controlled mouth. A disciplined face. Occasionally a hard one. Now unexpectedly tender.

"I meant to. And then —"

"Well? Go on. I don't bite little girls with eyes like black velvet pansies."

"It was because — well, Oorth said he'd give the — the other one — a deadline until noon tomorrow — today, that is. And then, right afterwards, you told me to go away — on the noon train."

Don stood watching her, his eyes alert, his expression puzzled. Then, unexpectedly, he gave a shout of laughter, leaned back against the kitchen table roaring, doubled up like a schoolboy. At length he sobered.

"Oh, no, Julie! You little goose. I told you to take the noon train because it's the only southbound train there is. And you'd come close to death twice. I wanted you safe. And you actually thought —"

Under his intent gaze she turned away. "Well," she blinked tears from her long lashes, "what would you have thought?"

"I know." He smiled and the cloud lifted from her heart. "Now tell me again exactly what happened to you this afternoon and exactly what you overheard."

Julie did. Don let out an exclamation like a low growl. "You didn't tell me *that* before! You mean you were deliberately pushed? That's why you came hurtling down that hill headlong, almost under the tractor!'' His face was white. He dropped the towel and caught her in his arms, his cheek resting on her hair. Julie could feel the hard pounding of his heart. She had not known that a man's arms could be so comforting. She wanted to press her cheek against his cheek, to float on this moment. Instead, she forced a gay laugh.

''Hey, look out,'' she protested. ''I'm getting soapsuds on your shirt.''

Don released her. ''Now,'' he said, ''tell me the whole thing over again.''

''Not again,'' she wailed.

''From the beginning.''

She did so and when she had finished Don expelled a long uneven breath. ''Thank God!''

She looked up in surprise. ''Why? What did I tell you this time that I forgot before?''

''It's only your tangerine ski suit that was seen. Not your face.''

''Why, yes — but —''

''Don't look like that,'' he said tenderly. ''It will be all right.''

''It won't be all right,'' she said unsteadily. "You think that whoever pushed me might — try again, might think I recognized —"

"Steady. I want you to promise me two things, Julie. Don't wear that ski suit again; keep it out of sight. And don't speak of this to anyone. Not anyone at all. Promise?"

She nodded.

He took a step toward her. Stopped. "Now off to bed with you," he said briskly. "You've had a terrible day. But don't think it is always like this in the woods. There are days when the air sparkles like wine and the beauty and the stillness catch at your heart. It's a wonderful place to live in. Good night, my darl — good night, Julie."

VIII

GOOD NIGHT, my darl — my darling, Don
had started to say. Stopped. Julie closed
the door of her bedroom and then, for the
first time in her life, locked it. She
switched on the light, took off the cherry-
red dress she had chosen — was it years
ago? — slipped on a green velvet robe
with a quilted lining and soft matching
slippers.

She was so tired she felt dazed, unreal,
but she could not go to bed. Her nerves
were pulled as tight as violin strings and
vibrated as though a master's fingers
pressed them.

The sleet beat a tattoo against the windows, the wind howled. There was a sharp
report, almost like a gunshot, as a limb
snapped under its weight of snow and the
terrible force of the wind. Somewhere

Lester was cowering under that killing wind, or had he already succumbed to the cold? Had he found shelter? Each shriek of the wind seemed to be a man's voice calling for help, each icy blast seemed to chill the girl's own slender body as her imagination pictured the fugitive.

Even if it were true — as Oorth had seemed to believe — that Lester had felled the tree across the road deliberately, he had not meant to harm her. She had been sure of that when she saw his face as he ran out of the woods. Perhaps he was like a young cousin of hers who was always getting in trouble because he never foresaw the consequences of what he did. Or had he intended to kill Oorth?

Again she heard in her mind that whispered conversation. Was it Lester who had said, "I'll kill you first?" Lester who had given her that terrible shove that had so nearly sent her to a horrible, mangling death?

She walked up and down the room, the green velvet train swirling behind her, until her knees gave way from sheer exhaustion. Then she dropped onto a chair at the small desk and snapped on the light. She had reached for paper and pen before she was aware of her own intention. She dipped the pen in the inkwell and wrote, ''Dear Quentin . . .'' Stared unseeingly at the paper.

Why had she turned instinctively to Quentin as though to a refuge not only from the horrors of the day and evening but from the memory of Don's arms around her? Because Quentin had always been there, a little stolid, a little unimaginative, but reliable, to be trusted. She had known him all her life, his personality held no surprises for her, his mind no secret places. And she did not know Don Bruce.

That was what troubled her, then. Might as well face it. Don't run away from the truth, Julie, she told herself. You are responding too fast, with a feeling Quentin never stirred in you, to a man about whom you know nothing. A man whom Newton Brewster called dangerous and Quentin described as a buccaneer.

She looked at the blank paper for a long time, noticing idly how bare her left hand looked without the big emerald ring Quentin had given her. Then she wrote a brief note to say that she had arrived safely and that she was glad she had come. Her aunt had too much responsibility to carry alone. And that, after all, was true enough. But she did not tell Quentin that a man lay dead in the cabin behind the lodge, a man who had died of violence. She did not tell him about the tree that had demolished the sleigh in which she had been riding, or about the shove that had pitched her headlong down a mountain side and almost under the gigantic wheels of a tractor. If she did, he would take the next plane and demand that she go home, and Julie discovered that she did not want to go home.

Home meant New York and a round of engagement parties; it meant fittings for her trousseau and shopping with Quentin for the duplex penthouse. It meant a big wedding in April, a honeymoon in Bermuda. It meant Quentin — forever.

She dropped the pen, chin resting on her clasped hands, and looked into the future. That would be what I've expected all my life. Looked forward to. Then why does it seem so — so gray? So drab? The girls I've known who were engaged were radiant, excited, their eyes filled with dreams.

But you can't dream dreams about

Quentin, she groped on. He would think it was silly. He wants me to be sensible, down to earth. A meek little woman for whom he will make all the decisions.

"It's a wonderful place to live in," Don had said about the Maine woods. A wonderful place to live in. She tried to push the words away, and the sound of his voice.

It wasn't wonderful; it was frightening. It was dangerous and threatening. At this moment Lester, if he still survived the storm, did not think it was wonderful. Or poor Swen Oorth.

Sudden death. Those had been Newton Brewster's words. *All the ingredients are there for battle, murder, and sudden death.* And he had been right. Impulsively, she wrote a brief letter to him, describing the murder of Swen Oorth, the hostility of the village and of the loggers to the Blaine camp, the disappearance of Lester. All that she withheld were her own narrow escapes from death. If he knew about them he would never let her stay. After all, hadn't he urged her not to come here in that telephone call just before she left New York? As though it were a casual afterthought, she concluded by asking him what he knew about a man named Don Bruce who had become Aunt Deb's new manager.

When she had sealed the letter she felt oddly relieved. She could sleep now. She opened the window the smallest crack and the sound and fury of the storm seemed to redouble.

Somewhere there was a faint reflection like that of light on snow. Julie watched it, puzzled. Was the light streaming from one of the windows on the first floor? She had assumed that Don would follow her upstairs, that he had gone to bed. Surely all the downstairs lights had been turned off. Had someone gone down again without her hearing?

In spite of the bitter cold, she flung up her window and leaned far out, sleet beating on her face and hair and the back of her neck. The light was not reflected from a window in the lodge. It came from the little cabin, just beyond the kitchen, which had belonged to Swen Oorth. For a moment the rectangle of a window in the cabin was revealed and then the light moved on. Someone inside was using either a flash or a lantern.

Hadn't Don said that he had locked

Oorth's cabin so that nothing could be disturbed until the State Police arrived to search it? Who could be down there, in the blizzard, with the dead man in that chilly cabin?

The light shifted again, revealed an open door. A dark shape loomed behind the light. Something drew up the eyes of that dark figure to Julie's window. She pulled her head in, jerked down the window, closed the drapes, ran to turn the switch. But she knew she was too late. Whoever had been in Swen Oorth's cabin had had plenty of time to check on the location of her lighted window.

There's nothing to be afraid of, she told herself. It isn't as though I had seen the prowler. I don't even know whether it was a man or woman. I'm no danger to him — or her. Yes, but does he or she know that? She wished she had not pulled the hangings shut in her panic, that she had waited to see what became of that dark figure behind the moving light. Perhaps it was Lester who had crept back for shelter to the one place where no one would be apt to look for him.

Perhaps — there was movement somewhere, a stair creaked. Someone coming up! I locked my door, she told herself. *Didn't I?* She couldn't remember. She groped her way through the dark room to the door, turned the knob and pulled. It was locked. She drew a little sigh of relief that caught in her throat. Then, under her relaxed hand, she felt the knob turn! Someone was trying to open the door. . . .

Helplessly she stood leaning against the panel, as though her slender strength could keep out the prowler who intended to force his way in. Under her hand the knob turned, turned again. Then it slipped back into place. Under her foot she felt a board move as someone stepped on it. It settled back into place. Then down the hall somewhere a door closed softly.

Too frightened to turn on the light, Julie groped her way to the bathroom for a big towel and rubbed her hair and face and neck dry from the sleet that had soaked them. Then she climbed into bed and pulled the covers high above her neck, burrowing deeper into her pillow, as wave after wave of fear swept over her. Deadly fear.

After all, the State Police did not arrive at dawn. The ringing of the telephone awakened Don Bruce who reached for the bedside light and looked at his watch. Six-thirty. It was still dark but the wind was down. The phone rang again. He reached for dressing gown and slippers and went down to the office to answer it.

''Don Bruce speaking.''

The voice at the other end spoke quickly, concisely, explaining the situation, giving orders, while Don's face grew more somber and new lines seemed to be etched in it.

At length he said, ''Okay, I'll carry on here as well as I can until you get through. . . . Nothing new except that one of the loggers has disappeared. He was heard to threaten Swen Oorth . . . . We searched for him last night. No trace at all. . . . Holed up somewhere, probably. . . . No, he can't be hiding in the village. The people there wouldn't help anyone from the Blaine lodge. . . . Well, that's another complication. It appears that the former manager was probably killed deliberately by someone here at the lodge.

One of the hunting rifles collected by Mr. Blaine disappeared from its rack in the gameroom the day of his murder. He was a resident of the village and very popular. The rumor is that the Blaine personnel are deliberately covering up. . . . I can manage, but I'll be relieved to see you. I have a feeling it's not all over, here.''

Don set down the telephone and stared at it bleakly. The blizzard had piled up snowdrifts that a snowplow could not clear for hours. The State Police were indefinitely delayed. So it was up to him to deal with people whose nerves were already stretched to the snapping point.

He went quickly up the stairs of the still-sleeping house, dressed and went down to the kitchen. He opened a cupboard, found coffee, measured it into the coffeemaker, thanking heaven that the electric power had not failed, that the oil burner still functioned and that the telephone was in working order. All in all, things might be a lot worse.

He poured a cup of coffee and sat down at the table with its red-checked cloth. Last night Julie had been in the kitchen with him. They had washed dishes together. That was when he had seen that the emerald was still missing. She had meant it, then, when she had pushed it across the table to Quentin that night in the New York restaurant.

His heart had leaped at the sight of her bare hand. She was free! And he had, he told himself in disgust, nearly lost any chance he might have had by rushing things. What had possessed him to tell her that this would be a wonderful place to live in? A girl like Julie would never be satisfied with a simple life. And yet her aunt had accepted it, gladly, for the sake of a man she had loved.

Whoa, he warned his galloping thoughts. The girl didn't trust you. Remember? Lovely as she is you wouldn't want her with the shadow of distrust between you. But think what it would be like to have her love and her trust, her gay companionship, the tenderness of which she is capable.

Stop thinking of it, he told himself sternly. You have a job to do. Stick to it. So far you have failed — miserably, completely. You have not found your man. Swen Oorth has been murdered almost under your eyes. Lester has slipped out of your hands.

He poured another cup of coffee. The night before they had searched as well as they could in the blinding blizzard, not daring to lose sight of one another. But, he had to admit, the search had been haphazard, inadequate. He set himself to remembering the terrain. Where could Lester have found shelter? Not in the logging camp itself; Keane and Wheeler had gone through that with a fine-tooth comb in spite of the sullen hostility and resentment of the loggers. There were a few sheds for tools and equipment, a stable for horses, an abandoned blacksmith shop. This morning they would try again.

Had Lester shot Oorth? Not, Don admitted to himself, if Oorth had been shot with the missing hunting rifle. None of the loggers ever entered the lodge. Unpalatable as the fact was, he had to acknowledge that the murder had been done by one of the three superintendents or by one of the two wives. Then why had Lester attracted attention to himself, drawn suspicion inevitably upon himself, by flight?

"What are you doing in my kitchen?"

Carrie stood in the doorway, wearing a crisp uniform, her face turned away to conceal the birthmark. Even with her face averted it was obvious that she had not slept. Her eyelids were red and puffy as though she had cried all night, and she was haggard.

"Good morning, Carrie. I was awakened by the telephone and decided not to go back to bed, though we won't get to work early today. No one, as you know, got to bed before midnight or later. I hope you don't mind having me invade your kitchen but I longed for some coffee."

Her face softened. "I don't mind. You aren't like the rest." She tied a fresh apron around her waist. "I'll have your breakfast for you in a few minutes."

"Sit down and have some coffee with me first," he suggested. "You look as though you hadn't slept well."

"Slept!" The word was bitter on her lips but after a fractional hesitation she filled a cup with steaming coffee and sat down across from him at the table, one hand creeping up to cover the scarred cheek. "I came down early to clean up the kitchen," she explained. "Miss Ames sent me to bed last night before the dishes were done. But someone has already washed them."

Don grinned and made a mock bow. ''I was the busboy and Miss Ames did the washing up.''

''I might of known,'' she sniffed. ''Neither of the other women would think of anyone but themselves. Miss Ames is going to be like her aunt and there aren't any finer people than Mrs. Blaine. Of course, Miss Ames is more beautiful than her aunt ever was. She hasn't the perfect features of Mrs. Keane but she's warmer, sweeter, more alive, somehow.''

''She's all of that,'' Don agreed.

He busied himself lighting a cigarette, careful not to look at this tragic woman who was so pitifully conscious of her disfigurement. Why did he think of her as tragic? While she measured sugar into her cup he risked a quick glance. It was not tragedy, it was despair that had ravaged her. He remembered her savage outcry the night before, ''He's being framed!''

Was that it? Was she suffering at the thought of the big redheaded logger freezing to death out in the storm? What was Lester to her? Why did she have so much faith in him?

He spoke gently, ''I'm worried about Lester.''

A spasm twisted her mouth. "You ought to be. Driving away an innocent man. Trying to pin Oorth's murder on him when the Lord knows there were plenty who had more reason to kill him than Lester did."

"Was Lester working here when the first manager was killed?"

"Yes, but so were all the others." A look of triumph came over her face. "But no one can accuse Lester of killing Downing. He was in town all that day getting supplies and playing cribbage with a friend where he stayed the night."

"I thought," Don said idly, "that Downing was killed in a hunting accident."

Carrie sniffed. "That's what some people wanted us to think. But what happened to the hunting rifle that was in the game-room that morning? I know it was gone because I dusted the rack with my own hands. That's what I'd like to know."

Don leaned toward her, his face grave. "You said there were other people with a motive for killing Oorth. Would you like to add anything to that?"

Carrie's swollen eyes met his with a level look. "Why not?" she said. "Take those two women. Oorth's been making passes at both of them. They are idle and they have nothing to do with their time and they've been flirting — to put the best light on it — with him because he was a single man and he liked women. Thought he was fatal to them.''

''Hugh Gordon is a bachelor, too,'' Don reminded her, ''and he seems to me much more attractive than Oorth.''

''He is more attractive in a way,'' Carrie admitted. ''But in the first place he didn't pay much attention to the wives, beyond being courteous, and in the second place Oorth had a bold sort of way that was more exciting to them. Gordon acts to me like a fellow who was kinda mother-spoiled. He feels sorry for himself and women don't like that so much. I don't mean that Clarisse Wheeler wouldn't flirt with any man in sight but Gordon kept out of the way of trouble. He could see what she was like. Anyhow, he spent his free time talking and joking with the men. They all like him a lot.''

''But the women, as I understand it, like Oorth.''

''I've seen both of them in his cabin, one time and another. They were jealous of each other. Anyone could see that. And jealous of Oorth. And besides that, there's their husbands. Neither Wheeler nor Charlie Keane looks to me like the kind of man to sit back while another man tries to take his wife away from him. So there's four suspects for you right now."

The cup rattled in shaking fingers as she tried to set it on its saucer. "Don't you see, Mr. Bruce, they've got more reason than Lester had for hating Oorth? He's just being made the scapegoat. He's innocent, I tell you. I know him better than anyone else does. He's innocent!"

"But," Don pointed out, "guilty or innocent, we've got to find the man. He can't live without shelter. If he survived the blizzard last night —"

Carrie's lips twitched in what was a mocking smile. The smile faded. Don's eyes were alert. The Bruce luck again! Carrie knew where Lester was; she was not afraid he was lost in the storm, only of what might happen if he were caught.

"Personally," he went on, "I don't believe Lester killed Oorth. But as long as he stays hidden he'll be regarded as guilty. That's why he was a fool to run away."

"If he'da stayed, he'da been killed next," Carrie said shortly.

"What makes you think that?"

"I know it's true." Carrie's eyes avoided his, her lips were pressed tight together.

"If he comes back, I'll protect him," Don told her. Then he waited, forcing himself to be patient, aware that any attempt to hurry her might simply silence her altogether. Somehow or other, he must win her confidence.

Carrie drank her coffee slowly, her eyes boring into his face. "How do you know," she demanded, "that you can protect Lester?" At length she nodded, "There's truth in you. And strength. There's great daring and there's kindness. I'd like to trust you but" — her voice broke — "God forgive you if you cheat me. I'm that frantic I don't hardly know where to turn."

"I can't protect him, of course, if he killed Oorth. You understand that?"

"He never!" the woman said fiercely.

"And," Don went on, "I can't clear him from the things he's been up to. He *has* been a ringleader in stirring up the men; he felled that tree deliberately to

153

block the road and nearly killed Miss Ames as a result.''

''He —'' Carrie faltered. Then she pushed back her chair, began to get food out of the refrigerator.

''I think he has already been punished for trying to block the road the villagers use,'' Don went on. ''He never meant to kill Old Molly. He liked that mare. And he never meant to endanger Miss Ames. But'' — he took his handkerchief and wiped his face — ''I hope I never again see anyone miss death by seconds as she did.''

''You're awful white!'' Carrie exclaimed.

''The trouble is that once you get off the track, you're apt to go farther than you meant. I think that's what happened to Lester. He got himself caught up in something too big for him.''

As Carrie started to lay a napkin on a tray he said quickly, ''I'll eat breakfast here, Carrie, if I'm not in your way.''

''What will you do if you find Lester?'' she asked. ''I'm telling you the truth, Mr. Bruce; he ran away so he wouldn't be killed next.''

''If he's innocent I'll persuade him to

tell his story to the State Police and clear himself.''

Carrie put fluffy scrambled eggs, sausage and toast before Don and refilled his coffee cup. She stood pleating her apron with nervous fingers. ''I don't know what to do,'' she wailed. ''I don't know what's right to do.''

IX

BY THE TIME the others had come down to breakfast, Don was in the office. He hailed the men as they passed the door and asked them to join him for a conference before setting out on the day's work. While he waited for them he went over the notes he had made for the State Police.

He thought again of Swen Oorth's body as he had seen it lying in the cabin, with a bullet in the head, scratches on the cheeks, pockets turned out. The whole picture was wrong. An attempt had been made to make the killing appear to be for the sake of robbery, but he felt convinced that it was mere stage setting, a red herring to cover up the real motive. Even for a billfold as well filled as the one Oorth carried, it would be madness to commit murder up here in the woods at the beginning of a blizzard.

Then, if it was not for robbery, was it to keep from paying blackmail? Five thousand dollars within twenty-four hours had been demanded by Oorth. Who would be able to procure that much money in so short a time? No one, so far as Don knew, but Florence Keane, who was a wealthy woman.

Don remembered Julie's report of her conversation with Oorth on their return from the station. Oorth had boasted that he knew what was going on. He had suggested that he would keep silent for a price. That did not sound like the jealousy motive.

Something big was at stake. An attempt had been made to kill Julie by shoving her down the hill so that she could not identify the whisperer. That meant that Oorth's murder had been premeditated, that the killer was prepared to eliminate anyone who endangered his own safety. God grant, Don thought fervently, the murderer does not discover that she owns the tangerine ski suit or Julie will be in terrible danger.

Heaven knew that he had done his best to persuade her to return to New York where she would be safe. He remembered Quentin's comment, which he had overheard, about her stubbornness, and his lips curved in a smile. Then he was grave again. Somehow or other, she had to be protected from the unknown menace that threatened her.

Memory flashed the picture of the deep scratches on Oorth's face. Whether or not jealousy seemed a likely motive for the crime, he could not overlook the evidence. Had those scratches been made by a woman's nails? If so, by Clarisse or Florence? If not, what could have produced them?

In the short week since his arrival at the Blaine lodge he had been aware that Oorth was playing with fire where both women were concerned. The man had seized every opportunity to ski with the lovely and enigmatic Florence Keane; he had exchanged meaningful glances and, Don had suspected, notes with the coquettish Clarisse. According to Carrie, both women had visited him in his cabin. Was that why he had insisted on private quarters? Had either of the women become enraged over his attentions to the other? Or had one of their husbands decided to put a stop to so intolerable a situation?

Suddenly the room was filled with blinding light. Don covered his eyes and then looked up, dazzled. He went to the window. The sun had come out and was blazing on a world encased in ice. The trees, the bushes, the ground were all one glorious spectrum of red, yellow, blue, green light. The loveliness was almost more than one could absorb.

He stood there enraptured, almost stunned, by the magic that had been wrought by nature's trick of congealing moisture. Each limb, each branch was encased in glittering ice; long icicles hung from trees and from the roof. The blinding beauty was unreal as some fantastic dream.

He forced himself to turn his back on that splendor, to focus all his attention on the immediate problem. Florence or Clarisse — which? Both women had reacted violently to Oorth's death, Florence by fainting, Clarisse by having hysterics. It was obvious that Florence had been afraid of the extent of her husband's jealousy. That was why she had cried out that he hadn't minded at all her skiing with Oorth. And yet Charlie Keane had drawn back from her touch as though it burned him.

Don had tried hard not only to sum up the men but to get below the surface in knowing them. He had succeeded better with everyone than with Charlie Keane. The latter was pleasant, likable, easy to get along with, but remote, not given to confidences, unusually reserved. What kind of man was he? Don had to confess to himself that he did not know the answer and yet that he liked him spontaneously more than the others.

Keane had married a woman who was both beautiful and wealthy, a woman, Don suspected, who was profoundly in love with her husband. And yet he had withdrawn from her. The previous evening he had chosen to play cards with Clarisse rather than go near his wife.

Clarisse Wheeler! Curtis had ordered her not to speak when she had lost her head over the news of Oorth's death. What had he been afraid that she would say? A big, hail-fellow-well-met type, the kind who joins a number of organizations and is a back-slapper. An overly self-confident extrovert. A good mixer . . .

It was not difficult to imagine Wheeler

beating Oorth up with his fists if he lost his temper. But it was more difficult to imagine him planning a murder cold-bloodedly, stealing the hunting rifle from the gameroom. Anyhow, it was too much to believe that there were two killers loose at the Blaine camp, and Wheeler had had no motive for killing Downing, the first manager. Or had he?

Don put his head in his hands. How glad he would be to see Holt of the State Police, to turn the matter over to someone who was trained to solve murders. He hoped devoutly, beautiful as the ice storm was, that it would not impede the police cars.

Now Wheeler came in looking alert and rested, his skin ruddy. "Any news of Lester?"

"Still missing," Don said briefly.

Wheeler grinned with amusement. "When do we start playing cops and robbers?"

There was no answering smile on Don's face. "We're playing it right now," he said, and Wheeler's eyebrows rose at his grim tone. "The State Police were delayed several hours ago by snow-drifts. How the ice storm will affect road conditions I shudder to think. Before the police come I want your statement, Wheeler.''

Wheeler chuckled. ''Nick Carter, the detective!'' He perched on the edge of the desk. ''And where was I when X marked the spot? That what you want to know?''

Don did not respond to Wheeler's amusement. ''Take it from about three o'clock yesterday afternoon.''

''Right you are, Sherlock,'' Wheeler said cheerfully. ''My gang was cutting up on the northeast corner. I was with them the whole time until we quit.''

''In sight of someone, all the time?''

Much of the confidence faded from Wheeler's face. ''Well — no. You understand how it is, Bruce. Men working at top speed. Don't notice anyone but the other guy on the saw. Moving around. You can't swear anyone was in a certain place at a certain time —''

Don nodded. ''Maybe we can narrow it down by questioning your gang. It will be a long job, though.''

''But —''

''Did you hear the dog howl?''

''Yeah. He sounded like a pack of wolves closing in.'' Wheeler cupped his hands to light a cigarette.

"Were you outside or inside at the time?"

"Out — in — I can't remember." Wheeler's good humor had faded; he looked sulky, on guard.

"Know anything about Oorth, anything that would make someone want to kill him?"

"He was a ladykiller," Wheeler snarled. "But I wouldn't have killed him, if that's what you are getting at; I'd just have kicked him good and hard." He laughed unconvincingly. "And if you think I was jealous because Clarisse was making eyes at him, you're nuts. She makes eyes at every man she sees and it doesn't mean a thing."

Then why were you so afraid she would talk last night?

The words shaped themselves on Don's lips but he held them back. Instead, he asked, "Ever come across Oorth when you were in Korea?"

"No, we weren't in the same outfit."

"Or the same prison camp?"

For a moment Wheeler's face was ugly. His lips drew back from his teeth in a snarl. "I wouldn't know. They had me in solitary most of the time because I tried to get away twice. Almost made it the second time. Oh, well —'' he tried to make his shrug careless but it didn't quite come off. Some of the corroding bitterness of that experience was revealed. ''It's over now. But, man, is it good to be out of doors! Tough on Clarisse, who likes the bright lights, but I've simply got to have a whole lot of space around me, room to swing my arms.''

Wheeler took a long, shaken breath. ''I don't ask anything better than to spend the rest of my life right here in the Maine woods. There's something about being penned up inside four walls that chokes me.'' He ran a finger under his collar as he spoke and then laughed at himself a trifle sheepishly.

''I know how you feel,'' Don told him. ''All right, Wheeler. That will do for now. Try to keep a sharp eye on your gang today. With Lester missing there's apt to be trouble. The whole lot of them seem to feel he is being framed.''

Wheeler's confidence seemed to come back to him. ''I can handle them,'' he said with assurance.

As he went toward the door with his

usual swagger, Don said casually, "Oh, by the way, Wheeler, what was it you threw down beside Oorth's body while we were in the cabin?"

Wheeler stopped with a jerk, was motionless for a space of several seconds. Then he said, "I didn't throw anything."

"Who did?"

"Search me."

He passed Charlie Keane who was coming into the office as he went out. Unlike Wheeler, the tall rangy man with the pleasant homely face looked as drained and haggard as though he had not slept for days.

"How's Florence this morning?" Don asked him.

Keane frowned. "She's all right," he said shortly. "A lot of fuss about nothing. I never saw such a woman for fainting. She's always doing it and it doesn't mean a thing."

Lie number one, Don thought with a sinking heart. You were scared out of your wits when your wife fainted last night. You're still scared.

Aloud, he explained briefly about the State Police and asked Keane to describe his whereabouts of the afternoon before.

Like Wheeler, Charlie was indefinite. He'd been with his gang but he couldn't prove it. They were busy, scattered through the woods, often out of sight of one another. In order to supervise them all, he'd had to keep moving from one place to another. Yes, he had been in his room when Monty howled. No, he didn't know of any reason why Oorth had been killed, didn't know of any enemies the man might have made.

His tired eyes were unexpectedly keen as he said abruptly, "I take it, Bruce, you don't believe Lester is our murderer."

Don made an evasive gesture but Keane laughed. "Nonsense, man! You wouldn't be hammering at us for alibis if you thought Lester was guilty. As a matter of fact, it wouldn't surprise me if you actually know where the fellow is. If you do, it seems to me it would only be fair to produce him."

Why was Charlie Keane so anxious to know about Lester? Don met the other man's eyes and there was ice in his blood for a moment. Carrie believed that Lester had run away to save his own life.

"I'm afraid I can't produce him," he said levelly. "I don't know where Lester

166

is. But until we have something like evidence of his guilt, a motive for killing Oorth, we can't let the matter rest there and assume his guilt.'' He leaned back in his chair. ''I'm at a disadvantage compared to the rest of you,'' he confessed.

''You see, I'm the late-comer. All the rest of you knew more about Oorth than I could find out in a single week. What was your opinion of him?''

''Unscrupulous,'' Keane said promptly, ''but good at handling the men. He was tough, but he worked along with them and though he wasn't exactly popular, something too sneaky about him, he had no trouble with his crew that I ever heard of.''

''Ever come across him in Korea?''

Unexpectedly, the warm attractive grin appeared on Keane's face. ''Not there — no. But I did see him in Tokyo on my first leave. You couldn't have missed him. Drunk, disorderly, disturbing the peace, and what have you. He got into trouble over some little Japanese girl whose parents complained to headquarters. An M.P. picked him up. Don't know what happened after that. I never laid eyes on the guy again until we both landed jobs here."

"You weren't in the same prison camp, I take it."

Keane's face drained of color. His lips were like parchment. He licked them. "I wouldn't know," he said, his voice hoarse. He started to take out a cigarette but his hand was shaking so hard that he put the package back in his pocket.

"Did you drop anything in Oorth's cabin last night?" Don asked, changing the subject abruptly. What had happened to Charlie Keane in the Communist prison camp? The possibilities turned him sick.

"Why no," Keane said, after a moment's hesitation. "No, I didn't."

Hugh Gordon was the last of the men to come in. Don looked up and smiled at the nice-looking youngster who stood hesitating in the doorway. "Come in, Gordon."

Hugh grinned as he sat down. "Gosh, who'd ever expect all this excitement in the Maine woods?" he said boyishly. "And to think I came here for peace and quiet."

"You didn't have much of that overseas, did you?" Don said quietly.

Hugh shrugged his shoulders. "Mrs.

Blaine says you were a prisoner like the rest of us so I guess I don't need to tell you what it was like."

"No," Don admitted grimly, "you don't need to tell me."

"And then," Hugh said, shaking his head, "of all places, I come up here and run into more Communist trouble."

"What Communist trouble?" Don asked sharply.

"Why, Lester, of course," Hugh said in surprise. "Didn't you know? He's been back of the labor unrest here, organizing the men. They talk to me quite a lot, you know."

"How did you find that out?"

"Well —" Hugh hesitated. "I've spent more time with the loggers than the other superintendents have. I didn't want to play around with Florence and Clarisse and have trouble with their husbands; and Oorth wasn't exactly companionable, so I've been pretty much on my own. The loggers are nice fellows, so I've spent most of my evenings playing checkers and gin rummy and chewing the rag, and helping a couple of them who are taking mail-order courses, trying to get an education."

169

"Nice work," Don told him. "You were here when the first manager died, weren't you?"

Gordon nodded his auburn head and smiled ruefully. "We all were. He was a good manager — though he did have it in for Lester. The poor guy died just five weeks ago."

"How did it happen?"

"A stray bullet from one of these amateur hunters. I don't know how some of these birds manage to get hunting licenses. They aren't safe." The boy looked at Don and his eyes widened. "You don't think —"

"I don't know."

"Whew! At least, with Lester dead in the storm, it must all be over. I can't pretend to be sorry."

"Dead?"

"No one could survive that blizzard." Hugh added slowly: "The poor guy! Though I've heard it is painless to freeze to death. You just lie down and go to sleep. I suppose he'll be found when the thaw sets in."

"I suppose so." Don took Hugh over his whereabouts the afternoon before, but again he found no real alibi. None of the superintendents had an alibi.

When Hugh had gone out to his gang of men, Don sat looking at his notes. He hadn't learned a thing except that no one at the Blaine lodge had a real alibi for Oorth's murder. Every man and woman was in the shadow of suspicion. Any one of them could have killed Oorth.

ii

The State Police arrived that afternoon. After hours of tension, Julie expected to feel nothing but relief; instead, her first sensation was one of alarm. What, she wondered, was she afraid of?

After the stark terror of the night, morning had brought sanity and courage. The brilliance of the light that drove away all the shadows and drakness and brought her a familiar world once more made her fear of the night seem incredible. And the sheer magnificence of the day made her repeat Don's words like a kind of chant: A wonderful place to live in. A wonderful place to live in.

She had come down to breakfast prepared to tell Don about the prowler in

Oorth's cottage, the prowler who had later tried to enter her room. But Don was in the office interviewing his superintendents and by the time she was sure they had gone she found the office empty. She had dropped her letters to Quentin Harrington and Newton Brewster into the tray for outgoing mail and gone back to join the other women.

After breakfast, Clarisse had followed her sulkily upstairs and again Julie had helped her to straighten up her room. It looked as disorderly as it had the morning before. Julie found herself looking on the dressing table for the small medal which had caused such tension the day before, but it was gone.

"Men," Clarisse grumbled as she tugged at the bedcovers, "are so selfish. Last night I begged Curtis to take me away from here. It's bad enough to have nothing to do and no place to go, but when someone gets killed?. . . And do you suppose Curtis cared how I feel? He wants to stay on and he just didn't pay any attention to me."

"Well," Julie said reasonably, "I don't suppose any of us would be allowed to leave until they find out who killed Mr.

Oorth.''

''Why not, I'd like to know,'' Clarisse said shrilly. ''They know who did it; that Lester who ran away.''

''Anyhow, your husband seems to enjoy his work. It would be a shame for him to have to give it up.''

''But what about me?''

''There's always someone for a woman like you,'' Florence said from the doorway. ''Why don't you try Don Bruce or Hugh Gordon?'' She laughed. ''Excuse me, I forgot that Don Bruce didn't seem to be interested.''

''Well, Charlie Keane did,'' Clarisse retorted maliciously. ''Plenty interested.''

''That's that,'' Julie said briskly, as she hung up the last of Clarisse's dresses. ''May I help you, Florence?''

She followed Florence Keane into her room and helped with the bed. There was no disorder in this room. ''Oh, how lovely,'' she exclaimed, as she saw the gold toilet appointments.

There was a frown between Florence Keane's perfectly arched brows. ''Lovely, yes,'' she admitted, ''but it was a mistake to bring them here. I've had the set so long I took it without thinking. I didn't realize how — out of place — as though I were flaunting all that gold.'' She rubbed the frown away, smoothed her brow. ''Sometimes,'' she went on, as though talking to herself, ''it seems to me I make more mistakes than anyone else.''

Julie laughed. ''You ought to hear a list of my blunders,'' she said gaily. ''They would fill a book.''

''But they wouldn't hurt anyone else,'' Florence Keane told her. Unexpectedly, the big brown eyes filled with tears. ''And Charlie has already been hurt enough. Something terrible happened to him in prison camp. He won't speak of it but I can feel it. And he won't tell me, won't share it with me; he bears it all alone. I don't know how to — reach him. And yet a shallow little fool like Clarisse has only to hold out her hand —''

''You know,'' Julie said impulsively, ''if I were you I'd ask him right out what's wrong. Reticence only seals it in. Maybe if he knew how much you wanted to help —'' her cheeks burned. ''I have no right to interfere,'' she apologized.

Florence leaned over and kissed her cheek. ''You are a sweet child. Perhaps you are right. Anyhow, there's nothing left to lose by trying it, is there?''

Something in the dreary hopelessness of her voice brought a lump into Julie's throat.

X

WHEN the beds had been made and the rooms straightened the three women went down to the gameroom by tacit agreement to stay with Mrs. Blaine, as though in need of mutual protection. Uncongenial as they were, none of them wanted to be alone. Mrs. Blaine, in silver-gray cardigan and skirt, was flanked by Clarisse in a scarlet slack suit and Florence in a beautifully cut violet wool, whose knowing simplicity meant an exclusive model. Crimson and gold flames in the big fireplace cut grotesque designs on the pine walls, on the half-finished puzzle on a table and on Julie's jonquil-yellow tweed as she perched on a green leather drum.

As the temperature rose and the sun beat on the ice, it began to melt, but the outside world was still glorious.

The men trooped back for lunch but the meal was a silent affair. The Keanes did not exchange a word. Clarisse and Wheeler quarreled in low, bitter tones. Don and Gordon were silent. The latter caught Julie's eye and winked at her.

Mrs. Blaine, who missed very little, commented, "He's an attractive boy. How do you like him?"

"So far," Julie reminded her, "your wilderness has provided so much excitement there hasn't been much time for conversation and getting acquainted. I've hardly exchanged a word with him yet."

"I don't want you to be bored."

Julie laughed outright. "Up to now," she declared, "I haven't been bored." Scared to death, horrified, tense with excitement, shaken by something in Don Bruce's eyes and the tone of his voice — but not bored, she thought.

Her joyous laugh brought the eyes of the three quiet couples to her face for a moment and Mrs. Blaine's expression of anxiety lightened.

"You'll never be bored," she agreed with a smile. "You love life too much. But you're young and I want you to have some amusement. Perhaps later —"

"There will be plenty to do," Julie assured her. "I'm going to learn to master those skis, and when the snow is cleared from the pond I'm going to skate. Besides, I need time for quiet; time to think —"

"To decide about Quentin?"

"About the future, at any rate." Julie's face sobered. "Somehow I don't think there's a place for Quentin in my future. I see more and more clearly the differences between us, the fact that we don't want the same things out of life. Quentin has his future all planned out, all part of a rigid schedule. He knows just what he wants to do, what he intends to accomplish by the time he is thirty and forty and fifty. There are no — surprises."

Her aunt's lips twitched with amusement. "Surprises," she pointed out, "aren't always amusing; and when you are building for life, they can be disrupting."

"Yes, but —"

"The important thing is how much your happiness depends on Quentin, on having him with you, on knowing that he is happy, helping to create his happiness." Mrs. Blaine smiled apologetically. "I'm trying to give advice and that's one subject on which it is dangerous to give advice.''

''Not yours, Aunt Deb,'' the girl said quickly, her lashes sparkling for a moment like the ice storm outside. ''Because yours is given out of love.''

''If love were always perfect wisdom,'' her aunt replied, ''there would be little suffering in this world.'' Her eyes wandered, as she spoke, to Florence Keane — who sat looking at her husband's expressionless, withdrawn face. Mrs. Blaine sighed.

''Things will be better now, Julie,'' she said, trying to be cheerful. ''Surely nothing else can go wrong.''

Julie responded to the anxiety in her aunt's voice. ''Of course it won't,'' she agreed with a great deal more optimism than she felt.

Within an hour, her optimistic words were proved wrong when the four men came trooping back to the house, looking frustrated and angry.

''What's wrong now?'' Aunt Deb asked, her lips white, her eyes moving from one set face to another.

''I'm terribly sorry, Mrs. Blaine,'' Don

told her, "but the men have gone on strike. They don't believe that Lester killed Oorth and they refuse to work until he is found and cleared of suspicion."

Julie looked quickly at her aunt, aware that the news meant disaster for her. If the timber were not cut by the first of April, she would be unable to meet her husband's debts. She would lose everything.

Mrs. Blaine took a long breath. "What can we do now?" she asked quietly.

Don took her hand. "You are a brave woman," he said gently. "There's only one thing we can do now and that is to wait for the State Police."

Clarisse whirled around. "If you aren't working, darling, for heaven's sake take me out skiing or something." She clung to Don's arm, looking at him from under her preposterously long artificial lashes. "I'll go crazy if I stay in here any longer."

Don stepped back so that her hand slipped from his sleeve. "Sorry, Clarisse. We'll all have to be on hand when the State Police arrive."

"But that may be hours," she protested. "If you can't go out, play gin rummy with me."

"Better ask Wheeler," Don said.

Curtis Wheeler let out a bellow of laughter. "Well, what do you know?" he crowed. "Here's one guy who is immune to your brand of charm, Clarisse."

She turned toward him, her sweet tones suddenly sharp and strident as she glared at her husband. "Oh, shut up!" Then she looked at Don. "It wouldn't be little Julie who has won your heart, would it?" Her tone dripped malice. "Because it won't do you much good. Look in the mailbox and you'll see that she is keeping a couple of guys in New York on the string while she's up here."

Julie flushed with anger. She was about to make a hot denial when she caught her Aunt Deb's eyes, with their cool detachment and their distaste for vulgarity. Her anger fell away and she shrugged her shoulders. For a moment Don's eyes sought hers and again she felt that electric experience she had known in the New York restaurant when she had not even known his name.

Florence, idly turning the pages of a magazine, had not moved since the men came into the gameroom. Her stormy eyes now sought her husband's face. There were depths in this woman compared to the shallow Clarisse. Unknown depths. Julie wondered if Charlie Keane had ever explored them or whether they remained a mystery to him.

They love each other, the girl thought, but they don't trust each other. It must be terrible to be married without trust.

Charlie Keane let himself down slowly in a chair beside Mrs. Blaine as though he were profoundly weary. He seemed unaware of his wife's intent gaze. He did not so much as glance in her direction.

To Julie's surprise, Mrs. Blaine turned to the tormented man the smile that made her young, a bewitching smile that held great sweetness. "Talk to me, Mr. Keane," she said, "if it won't bore you to chat with an old woman. I'm beginning to feel very lost and helpless."

Julie gave her aunt a quick, amused glance; she was, for all her appealing and fragile feminity, the least helpless woman Julie knew, but she was making a sure appeal to Charlie Keane. And Julie realized that the older woman was trying to draw him out of his abstraction and his gloomy thoughts.

He turned to her at once. "Old, Mrs.

Blaine?'' he protested. ''I wouldn't let anyone else say that of you.''

Hugh Gordon wrested Julie from her thoughts and pulled out a chair for her beside the half-finished picture puzzle. ''I don't know a darned thing about these puzzles,'' he admitted. ''But I'm not going to waste the first real chance I've had to talk to you. I want to know all about you.''

''Golly,'' Julie said with a ripple of laughter. ''That's a large order. Where do I start?''

Hugh laughed with her. ''Start at the beginning, go on to the end and then stop. All I know is that your name is Julie Ames, that you are Mrs. Blaine's niece, that you're the prettiest thing I've ever seen and —''

''Whoa!'' she said gaily. ''Do you always go as fast as this?''

His lips smiled but his eyes were earnest. ''How could I? I've never seen anyone like you before.''

For several minutes Julie had been dimly aware of the roar of a motor, the rattle of chains. Beside her chair Don said crisply, ''Sorry to break this up but the State Police have arrived.''

Julie look up in surprise. Why was Don Bruce so angry? His face was set. Compared with his firm maturity Hugh Gordon seemed very young, his mouth above the cleft chin was still indecisive, a boy's mouth. He flushed as Don glared at him and got quietly to his feet.

For a moment his fingers brushed lightly over Julie's hand. ''I guess it will have to wait until next time,'' he said, ''but, believe me, there will be a next time. And soon.''

Don still loomed over him, making him seem young and defenseless. Something in his manner aroused Julie's fighting qualities. He was ridiculously angry with Hugh simply because the boy was talking to her. She realized that Don was seething with jealousy. Deep down in her heart some feminine quality was pleased, but she did not reveal it. She gave Hugh a dazzling smile.

''Make it very soon,'' she said.

Don turned on his heel. Hugh's face lighted up. ''I will,'' he said eagerly and turned to look at the two men who had entered the room, one in plain clothes, the other in the uniform of the State Police.

The older man was in his middle thirties

with a long attractive face that looked tired. The other was a round-faced boy, trim in his uniform. He appeared to be about eighteen and was probably as old as Julie or Hugh Gordon.

The older man stood motionless, his eyes moving from face to face, resting on each deliberately but not impertinently, with the impersonality of a camera's eyes. As they left Julie she thought, I feel as though I'd been through an X-ray. That man wouldn't need to ask me, as Hugh did, to tell him about myself. He'd be able to tell me more than I've ever guessed about Julie Ames.

She watched his eyes complete their circuit. When they came to Don there was a flicker, a faint change of expression, and then they moved on. He recognized Don, Julie thought. Why didn't he say so? She looked at Don, saw that the sternness of a few moments before was gone, that he was more relaxed, obviously relieved to get rid of his heavy load of responsibility.

Belatedly, she realized what she had been searching for when the two men met, what had kept her keyed up all day. She had expected — feared? that the police officer's arrival would make Don nervous. She was conscious of a wave of shame of her own distrust and then of a glow of gladness. It's no use, she told herself, you can't run away from this any more, my girl. You can't escape being a part of whatever happens to Don Bruce. You're in love with the man. He is a stranger and you don't know anything about him, and you are the greatest goose alive, but you love him!

As though afraid that her sudden knowledge of herself would be betrayed by her face she turned away to look out of the window.

The older man picked out his hostess without hesitation and came toward her. ''Mrs. Blaine?''

''I am Deborah Blaine.'' She held out her hand with the gracious warmth that people found irresistible.

''I am Captain Holt of the State Police and this is Sergeant Smith.''

''You are most welcome here,'' she told him. ''I trust it isn't necessary to assure you that we will all give you every assistance in our power in clearing up this terrible tragedy.''

''Thank you, Mrs. Blaine. That ought

to be a great help. When people co-operate with their police forces, half our problem is solved.''

''This is my manager, Mr. Bruce. Captain Holt.''

The two men shook hands as though they were total strangers.

''I suggest,'' Mrs. Blaine said, ''that Mr. Bruce turn the office over to you for your own use while you conduct your investigation. When you are ready for us, we will be at your disposal.''

''Thank you. There's another car with me: fingerprint man, photographer and a doctor. Perhaps, Mr. Bruce, you will show us the body first.''

Don nodded and led the two men out the front door where the other members of the State Police staff were climbing out of their car. Silently they went around the house to the cabin that had belonged to Swen Oorth.

''Nothing has been touched, of course,'' Don said. ''I locked the place myself after I had made sure the man was dead.'' He took the key out of his pocket and turned it in the lock. Pushed the door open. Stood rooted in the doorway until Captain Holt impatiently nudged him to one side.

The room looked as if a mopping-up squad had been searching it for snipers. Drawers of a huge flat mahogany desk had been pulled out, two of them had landed on the floor. Their contents — packages of envelopes, boxes of rubber bands, paper clips — spilled from small cartons, littered the rug.

Records had been pulled from the cabinet and scattered. Whoever had been here had been in a frantic hurry to find something. Don's roving eyes came to rest on the outstretched figure by the fireplace. The bottom dropped out of his stomach. The body had been turned over so that the great hole in the back of the head was no longer visible. Now Swen Oorth's eyes stared blankly up at Don, the black hole between and just a little above them.

''Someone got in here last night,'' Don said at last, hoarsely. ''When we found the body, it was lying on its face. Nothing in the room had been disarranged. The phonograph was running, playing 'Home on the Range,' and we stopped it. That's all.''

Idly, the young sergeant looked at the open cabinet. ''There's no record on now,'' he said.

Don ran his hand through his hair. "I have the only key, so far as I know, and the lock wasn't forced. I don't understand —"

"You've run headlong into an idea," Captain Holt said, a look of amusement brightening his tired face. "I saw when it hit you."

"Well, there's a possibility that just occurred to me," Don admitted. "Carrie, the cook and housekeeper, has another key. She cleans the place, that is she cleaned it for Oorth, made his bed, and so forth. Extra service, of course. I don't know whether he paid her or — brought pressure on her."

"What sort?"

"I don't know."

"You think this woman wrecked the place?"

"No," Don said reluctantly, "but I suspect she gave her key to our missing logger, and he was the one who wrecked it. He couldn't have found a safer place to spend the night out of the blizzard. It's the one place we never thought of searching."

While the photographer and fingerprint

men got to work, quickly, efficiently, and almost without words, the doctor stooped down to examine Swen Oorth's still body.

Holt stood for a long moment, without moving, his eyes roving around the room. Then he nodded, gave some low-voiced instructions to his sergeant, and turned to Don.

"All right, Bruce, let's have the whole story. When you came to see me a week ago, before you took the job, I thought you'd got hold of a mare's-nest. But it begins to look as though you were right."

"I'm not sure," Don said slowly. "It's beginning to seem quite possible that Oorth's death has nothing to do with my own business; that it's a side issue."

Captain Holt's eyebrows shot up. "What makes you think so?"

"Those scratches on Oorth's face, for one thing," Don told him. "That looks as though there is a woman in the case. Of course, the scratches may have nothing to do with Oorth's murder. Frankly, I've never been so glad to see anyone in my life as I was to see you, Captain. I'm clear out of my depth."

"Not if half I have heard about you is true," the captain replied. "But let's have the whole thing." He looked up as the doctor got to his feet.

"What do you want me to tell you that you can't see for yourselves?" the doctor asked sourly. "Man's been dead since about six o'clock last night, so far as I can tell now by the condition of the body. I'll know more definitely about the time after the post-mortem. Shot though the head and died instantly. Probably a high-powered rifle. Curious murder weapon. And those scratches on his face were made before death."

He picked up his bag and went off. "Now then," Captain Holt said, "let's have it."

Don Bruce told him the whole story, beginning with his arrival the week before. He hadn't, he admitted, been able to come to any conclusion as to which, if any, of the four men was the one he was seeking. He had observed, however, that there was plenty of cause for trouble. Oorth was carrying on blatantly with the married women, whose husbands were ready to take him apart. There was also considerable labor unrest, which dated from the time of the death of the first manager, Downing.

Captain Holt nodded thoughtfully. "I knew Downing. He grew up in the village and he was a fine fellow. Everyone liked him. Never heard of labor trouble from any group he had anything to do with."

"I gathered that," Don said. He then repeated what Julie had heard from the stationmaster. "There's no doubt," he went on, "that the town people believe there was something wrong with Downing's death, that it was no mere hunting accident. And it looks to me as though they were right."

He told about the hunting rifle that had disappeared from the wall of the gameroom on the day of Downing's death and said that a second had disappeared the afternoon before, a few hours previous to Oorth's death.

Lester, the missing logger, Don went on, was involved in the whole thing. But it was difficult to tell to what extent. Hugh Gordon, the youngest of the superintendents, who had spent a lot of time with the men, believed Lester had been organizing them and that he was a Communist.

"Lester isn't," Don said, "the principal character here, I'm pretty sure of that. He is being used by someone. But he deliberately felled a tree to block the road the townspeople use and he came so close to killing Miss Ames —'' He steadied his voice and described the accident. Then he went on to relate Julie's experience on the hillside, the conversation she had overheard and the shove that had so nearly sent her under the treads of the tractor.

Something in his voice, in his white face as he talked, made the captain give him a keen look, but he made no comment. Obviously Bruce was crazy about the girl but that was no concern of his. Don went on to the howling of the dog Monty, to Hugh's discovery of Oorth's body and his own impression that one of the three superintendents had moved while they were in the cabin. Later he had found the queer-shaped medal lying beside the body.

He took it out of his billfold and gave it to Holt. The latter studied it carefully, turning it over.

''Never saw anything like it,'' he admitted. ''Might be someone's lucky piece — something like that.'' He held it closer to his eyes. ''There seems to be a tiny number scratched on one side — 876.

Perhaps the experts can tell us more about it.''

''Then,'' Don said, ''Lester disappeared. I'm pretty sure Carrie, the cook, knows where he is, but I don't think we'll get the information out of her by heckling. She'll just clam up. She believes, rightly or wrongly, that Lester ran away because he was afraid he'd be killed next. I've talked to everyone and there's not a human being here, with the exception of Mrs. Blaine, who is clear of all suspicion.''

''Well,'' Captain Holt said when Don had concluded his report, ''that's quite a story. Thank heaven, you were on hand to help me sort it all out.''

Don shook his head. ''I haven't been able to sort it out to my own satisfaction yet. I'm completely confused. I have suspicions but not a scrap of concrete evidence.''

''We'll see what the rest of them have to contribute,'' Captain Holt decided. He gave orders for the removal of Oorth's body and then went out of the cabin with Don. The latter took a long breath of the icy air outside, relieved to be free of those staring eyes looking sightlessly

194

from Oorth's dead face.

As he started to go around to the front door, Captain Holt stopped him. "I'd like a word with this woman Carrie," he said.

"All right, but watch your step. She doesn't trust any of us and she believes wholeheartedly in Lester."

Carrie was lifting a pie out of the oven as the two men went into the kitchen. She turned round sharply and nearly dropped the hot pan.

"Carrie," Don said quietly when she had placed a second pie beside the first one to cool, "this is Captain Holt of the State Police who has come to help us straighten out this mess. Mmm. Not apple pie!"

Carrie put up her hand to cover her cheek. She half smiled. "Yes, it's apple pie."

"My favorite," Don declared enthusiastically. "Hot apple pie with heavy cream on it. That is a dish for the gods."

"I was planning to serve it cold," she said. "Well," with a reluctant smile as she saw his look of disappointment, "there's plenty; I made big pies; I guess you could have some now."

Don beamed. "I don't like to crowd my

luck," he said, "but how about a piece for the captain? If he sees me eating hot apple pie with cream and he doesn't have any, he's apt to run me in, out of sheer jealousy."

Captain Holt nodded gravely. "If I saw you eating hot apple pie and cream when I didn't have any," he threatened, "I'd send you up for life."

Carrie laughed outright at their nonsense, and Don noticed in surprise that when she was gay she was almost pretty. It was a darned shame about the scar. Perhaps something could be done. He'd talk to Mrs. Blaine about it later.

While the two men ate and praised the pie, Carrie watched, flattered and smiling, her fear of the captain fading away, her tension relaxing. When she seemed to be completely at ease, Holt said, "I forgot to get a key for that cabin, Bruce. The place should be locked up, you know."

"That's right." Don did not refer to the key in his pocket.

"I have one," Carrie volunteered. "I keep it on the hook here in the kitchen." She reached for it and the two men, watching her, saw the surprise in her face. "It's gone!"

"That accounts for it then," the captain said in apparent relief. "Someone ransacked the place in the night. The prowler must have taken your key."

"You mean to say someone got into Oorth's cabin last night?" Carrie would have to be a better actress than seemed possible to pretend the surprise, the shock, she revealed.

"It might be this missing man, Lester," Holt said idly.

"It wasn't," Carrie snapped. "He wasn't near here last night. He —" her lips clamped tight together. Don knew that there was nothing more to be gained from pressing her at this moment. After an exchange of glances the two men thanked Carrie for the pie, went out of the kitchen, leaving her alone in her brooding silence.

XI

IN the firelighted gameroom shadows drifted across the pine walls. Night noises came through the closed windows. Julie lay back in her chair, feeling drained and depleted by yesterday's tragedy, a night of strain, and the impact of Captain Holt of the State Troopers on the superintendents and their wives. It seemed to her that Don had been the only person relieved by the arrival of the authorities. The others were afraid.

Clarisse huddled close to her husband. Wheeler was his normal self, the what-a-big-boy-am-I swagger was in full force. Earlier Julie had heard sharp words from the Wheeler room but now the couple was giving an impression of devotion. Julie wondered how much of their attitude of marital happiness was the result of

Wheeler's curt commands to his wife. Apparently he was anxious to convince Captain Holt that there was no cause for jealousy between him and Clarisse, that they were completely and happily absorbed in one another.

Florence Keane sat alone, her somber eyes on her husband's face. Charlie Keane was shuffling cards for his eternal game of solitaire. Earlier, Aunt Deb had talked to him for a long time, speaking in a low tone. Julie had heard little of that conversation but she had gathered that Aunt Deb was talking about what different creatures men and women were; how women needed to be reassured that they were loved and that they were often too proud to let the man they loved see their unhappiness.

"Sometimes," Julie had heard her say at one point, "I think half the broken marriages could be saved by honest speaking from the heart. When you consider all the misunderstandings that grow out of mistaken reticence — I remember once . . . ." She had laughed a little and launched into a gay story of a ludicrous misunderstanding with her beloved Jim. It was a good story and Charlie Keane had laughed outright when she finished it.

Julie smiled to herself. Darling Aunt Deb! Her own happiness was nothing but memories now, but she didn't surrender to her grief; she was trying to patch up the precarious happiness of others.

Hugh Gordon had curled up at Julie's feet; every now and then he tilted back his curly head to smile at her but, like the others, he could not bring himself to break the silence that hung heavily over the room.

Don Bruce was in the office with Captain Holt; the other men — photographer, fingerprint man, doctor — had gone some time before. Aunt Deb came in and the men got to their feet.

"Supper is delayed again," she said in a tone of resignation. "I don't know what's got into Carrie. I do hope you aren't starving."

Julie rose to her feet. "I'll help her," she offered.

"Just a moment, Miss Ames."

Captain Holt stood in the doorway. "I'd like to ask you a few questions, if I may, and then" — his smile lighted his tired face — "then you can help with the cooking."

Mrs. Blaine protested quickly, "My niece arrived only yesterday morning, Captain. She didn't know anyone here. She can't possibly be involved."

"I realize that, Mrs. Blaine," the captain replied in the gentle tone men instinctively used with her. "I won't keep her long."

"If you aren't back in ten minutes," Hugh laughed, "I'll call out the marines and come to the rescue."

Don, who had been sitting by the fire in the office, got up as Julie came in, followed by Captain Holt. The latter closed the door behind him and pulled out a chair for her.

"Now, Miss Ames, I want you to tell me everything you have seen and heard since you came up to the lodge."

"That's — rather a big order," she began unsteadily.

He leaned back in his chair, relaxed and at ease as though this were just a friendly meeting, and again Julie liked his long tired face. It occurred to her that he had been on duty the night before with no rest, but he was neither irritable nor impatient. He acted as though he had all the time in the world.

"I know it's a big order," he agreed, "but there is a lot at stake and every scrap of information is needed. I don't need to tell you that a killer is loose among you."

"But Lester —"

He shook his head. "Perhaps, but I don't think so. The blunt truth, Miss Ames, is that every soul in this house is under the shadow of suspicion."

Julie took a long breath and began to tell him what he wanted to know, starting with her arrival, the words the station-master had spoken to her, and the accident of the felled tree. The captain listened intently.

When she had finished, he took her back over the whispered conversation which she had overheard on the hillside. "Miss Ames," he said, and his voice was grave, more serious than she had heard it before, "you have too much character to panic. No one could see those eyes of yours and not know that you have a level head. I want to point out that you are in personal danger. Very real danger. Whoever pushed you is not going to rest until he or she finds out who owns that tangerine ski suit and how much you overheard of that conversation. Above all, whether he or she was recognized. After this, don't go off by yourself. Stay with other people.''

''But what other people?'' Julie asked, her voice shaking. ''If no one is free from suspicion, how can I tell whom to trust?''

''Tomorrow I'll get the sergeant back here,'' Holt told her, ''and make it his job to keep an eye on you.''

''Surely that isn't necessary,'' she protested.

''I wish it weren't.''

A chill shook her. This man was warning her that someone wanted to kill her, Julie Ames! It didn't seem credible.

''I'll take over the job until the sergeant gets here,'' Don said and Holt nodded approval.

Julie gave Don a little smile of gratitude and her heart glowed. There was someone whom the captain absolved from all suspicion — Don Bruce. Whatever the mystery in which he was involved, it was one that carried no discredit.

''And lock your door at night,'' Captain Holt said.

''I did that last night, thank heavens!'' Julie said.

The captain's gaze sharpened. ''What

happened last night that you have not told us?''

''Someone tried the door of my room. It was,'' she tried to laugh but did not make much of a success of it, ''rather scary.''

''When was this?'' Don asked.

''About a half-hour after we went upstairs.'' The soft color flooded her cheeks as she remembered his parting words, ''Good night, my darl —'' She turned to the captain to avoid Don's eyes for fear he would guess how shaken she was by that memory. ''I wrote some letters.'' She remembered Clarisse's taunt and again felt the color rush into her face. ''Anyhow,'' she rushed on rather incoherently, ''I was just going to bed when I heard a step on the stair and someone turned the knob.'' There was no color in her face now, just stark horror as she remembered that moment of terror. ''And I knew it was whoever had been in Oorth's cabin.''

''What!'' The two men sat bolt upright with an identical exclamation.

She told them, then, about the light that had attracted her attention, about the dark figure behind the lantern, and that the prowler had seen her lighted window. She had pulled the drapes together and shut off the light. But too late. In a few moments someone had tried her door. And after what had seemed like centuries had gone away again and a door had closed. She didn't know which one.

The captain's face was set. "You had a close call, Miss Ames."

Don was beside her, his hand on her shoulder. "Why didn't you call me?"

She gave a shaken laugh. "I'd have waked up everyone in the house and startled Aunt Deb. Anyhow, I don't believe I could have got a sound out. My throat was — frozen."

"Why didn't you tell me this morning?"

"I meant to tell you as soon as I came down to breakfast but you were interviewing the men and you've been busy ever since."

"Did you get any impression," the captain asked, "as to whether it was a man or a woman in the cabin?"

Julie shook her head. "It was only a dark blurry figure. I don't even know whether it was tall or short. Just a figure."

The captain opened his hand. On the palm lay an odd-shaped medal. "Have you ever seen that before?" he asked.

Julie's eyes widened. "Why, yes, I have."

"Where?"

"I don't know."

"Try to think, Miss Ames; it may be very important."

Julie shut her eyes, trying to recall where she had seen that medal before. Then she remembered. "It was on —" she broke off, startled.

"That won't do," the captain told her firmly. "You must not withhold information from the police."

"It was on the dressing table in Clarisse Wheeler's room," she said reluctantly.

"You're still holding something back," Holt said shrewdly.

"Well, I noticed it because Florence Keane was in the room and she gave a kind of gasp and I saw she was looking at the medal, that she recognized it. Then she looked at Clarisse and Clarisse laughed, sort of triumphantly. That's all I know. And maybe I read too much into it, gave significance to something that had no real meaning."

"All right, and thank you, Miss Ames. Don't mention that medal to anyone else.

And now," the captain was nice when he smiled, "you are free to get supper and you'll win the eternal gratitude of all of us."

When she had gone there was a moment's silence. Then the captain got up from behind the desk, put away his notebook, took out a pipe and came to join Don beside the fire. He smoked thoughtfully. At length he leaned forward to knock out his pipe.

"Major Bruce," he began unexpectedly and Don looked up startled. "Sorry, I forgot for the moment that you act unofficially for the Department —"

"You seem to know a great deal about me," Don commented.

"With murder in my territory, I look into everyone's credentials," the captain told him grimly. "Major — Mr. Bruce, if you prefer, when you came to see me a week ago you were pretty vague about what your real mission was at the Blaine lodge. I didn't ask questions then, because I thought your problem had no connection with my duties. Now I am not so sure. How much can you tell me?"

Don deliberated. "I don't see," he replied slowly, "why I can't tell you the whole thing. If it proves to have nothing to do with these murders, I know it will be safe with you. And it will be a big help to be able to talk the thing out, help me to see it more clearly."

The captain nodded without speaking. In the course of a few hours, the two men had acquired mutual respect and trust and the beginning of a rare friendship, which needed no words.

Don leaned forward, his lean, well-cared-for hands clasped around one knee. "As you know," he said, "the superintendents and I have two things in common: we are all Korean veterans and we were all Communist prisoners."

The captain nodded. "There has been a lot of talk around the community about Mrs. Blaine making a place here for the ex-service men who had most suffered for their country. At first, there wasn't a thing people wouldn't have been glad to do for her. And yet, lately, there is nothing but hostility at the very mention of the Blaine camp."

Don said thoughtfully, "There were, of course, a huge number of United Nations prisoners, quite a few of whom were Americans. At times," he brushed his hand over his eyes, "I thought I'd never see this country again. The situation was — unspeakable. They tried everything: hard labor, starving, freezing, abuse — but the strongest weapon they had was propaganda; that is," he corrected himself, "it was a strong weapon with weak men, inadequate men, those with a sense of grievance because they had never learned to adjust to their environment and so blamed circumstances instead of themselves for their personal failures.

"Well, the unforgettable day came when some of us were released. And that day, when I was being checked out, a little conference was taking place behind the thin walls of the prison building. The conference was in English. One of the men spoke with a heavy accent. The other one mumbled. That one had — sold out. He was coming back to America ostensibly as a man glad to be free from prison, actually as a Communist organizer."

The captain sat erect with a muffled exclamation.

"I got the names of the group being released that day. They were," Don added deliberately, "Swen Oorth, Hugh Gordon, Charles Keane and Curtis

Wheeler. I never saw the men. But one of them is a traitor and, heaven help me, I can't figure out which one it is.''

''You never saw him at all?''

''There were cracks in those walls and the man who was checking me out had left his desk for a few minutes. That's how I happened to overhear the conversation. Otherwise he'd have warned them or silenced me altogether. All I saw was a fellow so huddled over that I couldn't even make out his size. And I heard a few words so muffled I couldn't distinguish the voice.''

Don stretched out his legs to the fire, forced himself to relax. ''When I landed in California I got in touch with Washington by telephone and was instructed to track down my man. I followed various leads, heard of a place in San Francisco's Chinatown which was a headquarters for Communist activities on the coast, and went there for dinner. I got a hot lead, thought I had my man — and he escaped by a back door. At that point I thought my luck had failed and I had lost all trace of him.''

He bent over to stir the fire. ''I've studied those four men until I nearly went mad this past week. And I simply don't know. At first, I had my eye on Swen Oorth because he was handling too much money and he was obviously a bad one. Whichever one it was would be provided with ample funds for his work here. Curtis Wheeler has a wife who makes constant demands on him and he'd never be able to satisfy them out of his salary. To make matters worse, if he won't give her what she wants, she'll try to get it from other men. That's motive for you.

"Then there's Charlie Keane who married a woman with a lot of money though he has none himself. She's a beautiful creature, as you've seen for yourself, and he may have felt he had to have as much money as she has to hold his own." The frown deepened between Don's eyes. "Something went very wrong for Keane while he was in prison camp. His reaction to his experience is worse than that of any of us, though none of us found it a bed of roses. I can't get at the root of his trouble. Whether he joined the Party over there and regretted it later, and found that he couldn't get out — I just don't know."

Holt tapped out his pipe on the hearth, his eyes still on Don's face, taking in

211

every word.

"That leaves young Hugh Gordon. He seems to be a nice kid and he's trying hard to make good on the job. The loggers like him. I don't know much about him, though he's talked about himself to Mrs. Blaine. She may have learned something I haven't got. But what bothers me now is whether the murders of Downing and Swen Oorth have anything to do with my problem or whether they are outside it entirely. Certainly, those scratches on Oorth's face look like a woman's work, and the medal tossed down beside his dead body, the medal Julie saw among Clarisse's things, looks as though it were a crime of passion and jealousy rather than of politics."

"How did you get on the track of these men after losing the trace in Chinatown in San Francisco?" the captain asked.

Don grinned. "The Bruce luck. I'd lost them entirely and then I went to a restaurant in New York. Julie Ames was sitting at the next table with Newton Brewster, who had just been up here to visit her aunt. I heard him mention the names of the superintendents and say that Mrs. Blaine needed a manager. I sent a telegram applying for the job that night and later got in touch with Brewster and told him my story. He decided that it would be better not to let Mrs. Blaine know because of her bad heart.''

''Doesn't it strike you as rather an amazing coincidence that all your suspects should turn up here?'' Holt asked.

''Well, no. There was a lot of publicity when we were freed, you may remember, and Mrs. Blaine just made her offer to the whole lot.''

''It looks as though you have your job cut out for you,'' Captain Holt remarked.

''And how! The men have gone on strike to protest against Lester being driven away, as they put it. In my opinion, Lester has been someone's tool. Now that he has served his purpose and suspicion has fallen on him for Oorth's murder, I am afraid that he is in danger. It would be most convenient for someone if Lester were to appear to be guilty of the murders, and then be found dead of exposure so he couldn't clear himself. I'd give a lot to make Carrie talk, to make her realize that we can protect him better than he can himself.''

''Heard any comments that give you

some idea of how the superintendents stand in regard to Lester?''

Don ran his hand through his hair. ''Only one — Charlie Keane, again. How he keeps cropping up in this investigation! He was the first to see clearly that we weren't regarding Lester very seriously as our criminal. He suspected I knew where he was and tried to get the information out of me. I didn't like it at all because — well, I like Keane.''

When Julie left the office she went out to the kitchen. Carrie was busy at the stove, a towel tied around her face.

''What's the matter? Toothache?'' Julie asked sympathetically.

Carrie nodded.

''I've come to help you,'' Julie said. ''What are you planning to serve?''

''I can manage all right,'' Carrie said so quickly that Julie thought in a flash: She doesn't want me here; she's up to something and she wants to be alone.

''I'll peel the potatoes,'' she said — tied on a big apron and got to work. While she was busy at the sink she watched Carrie in the small mirror over her head. Yesterday it had been headache, today toothache. Carrie was deliberately malingering, she was sure of that. The headache had been an excuse to get away from the kitchen at the time when Lester disappeared. The toothache — Julie's heart leaped. Lester might have found a shelter from the storm but he needed food. Carrie must know where he was, she must be planning to take food to him.

If I can only hold her off until it's time to serve supper, she thought, she will have to postpone her trip until after the meal is served because she'd be missed at once. Julie talked gaily while she worked but all the time her mind was busy. Carrie had obviously been on the point of slipping out of the kitchen when Julie had appeared. That meant she must already have the food prepared. As soon as Carrie left the kitchen to set the tables Julie looked around, opening cupboard doors, searching quickly. Carrie came out as she was looking on a high shelf. She got off the folding ladder, her face flushed.

"I want some of Aunt Deb's watermelon pickles," she said. "I thought they were kept up here."

"All the stores are kept in the basement now," Carrie said. She looked startled.

The sight of Julie checking over the cupboard shelves had been a bad shock.

"I'll get them for you," Carrie offered. "You go in the other room. And thanks for helping."

Julie took her apron off slowly, taking so much time that the meal finished cooking and, in desperation, Carrie carried the soup tureen into the dining room. She couldn't leave now. Then at last Julie bent over to open the cupboard under the big sink. There was a basket containing two "Thermos" bottles and packages done up in wax paper. She closed it quickly, her face flushed with excitement. You've got to tell Don or Captain Holt as soon as supper is over, she thought — and found that she dreaded doing it, as though she were being treacherous to this unhappy woman, as though she were a bloodhound on the trail of the fugitive.

She straightened up as she heard Carrie's returning footsteps. There was no time to move away but she looked into the mirror above the sink, rearranging her soft waves.

Behind her Carrie spoke abruptly. "What is it like to be beautiful?"

"Why I —" Julie turned to face her,

at a loss for words.

"All the men were swept right off their feet when you came here, and the women were jealous. And Mr. Bruce — anyone can see what happened to him. Mr. Gordon, too. What's it like, Miss Ames, to have people like to look at you?"

"Carrie! Poor Carrie!" Julie put her arm around the woman's shoulder. "Do you know, Carrie, that you are a pretty woman?"

Carrie jerked away in anger.

"Good heavens," Julie cried, "you can't think I am joking. But that scar — it could be covered entirely up by a skin graft."

Carrie's eyes widened in almost incredulous hope. "It could?"

"I'm almost sure."

A reddened, work-worn hand clutched at her sleeve. "And a man could look at me without — without pity?"

"Of course."

The tears welled from Carrie's eyes. "You can't know what it's like to be me. I never had dates like other girls. No one ever paid any attention to me. And yet a woman's heart is made for loving, Miss Ames, even when she is plain, even when she is ugly, as I am. She just has to love someone or part of her dies.''

She wiped her eyes with the back of her hand. ''It was at church in town that I met Lester. And he was kind. Real kind. He took me to the movies and to church suppers and he came to see me now and then. And I would have died for him. Though it was only pity. I knew that. And I won't let them hurt him.''

She glanced at the kitchen clock and was startled. ''I'd best tell them supper is served,'' she said hastily. ''It's getting late.''

XII

BY THE TIME Julie reached the gameroom Carrie had announced supper and there was a general move toward the door. Julie caught Don's attention and he joined her, a question in his eyes.

When the others had gone out he asked quietly, ''What is it, Julie? I thought you had eyes like black-velvet pansies but they are so big now I'll have to think of some other flower.''

''It's Carrie,'' she said almost in a whisper. ''I'm sure she knows where Lester is hiding. I think she is planning to smuggle food out to him tonight. There's a hamper with 'Thermos' bottles and sandwiches hidden under the sink. And she is pretending to have a toothache, getting ready to leave. She was watching the clock so I'm pretty sure she has an appointment, that she is expected at some particular time. I'm afraid for her, Don. If Lester did kill Swen Oorth, Carrie shouldn't be trying to see him. Suppose he began to worry for fear she'd tell someone else. Suppose —"

He nodded, his face grave. "You are right," he decided. "We'd better keep an eye on her and make sure she doesn't leave the house alone. She'll probably lead us straight to Lester."

"That's what I thought." Julie's eyes were troubled. "Don, do you think we're doing something terribly dishonest? Carrie would never forgive me if she knew."

"Don't be absurd," he told her. "You are only trying to protect her. We'd better join the others in the dining room now."

When she entered the dining room Julie found that changes had been made in the seating arrangements. Captain Holt had taken Hugh Gordon's seat at Don's table and a third chair had been placed there for Mrs. Blaine, who was playing hostess as though the State Policeman were an honored guest and his presence purely a social one.

Hugh Gordon had Mrs. Blaine's seat across from Julie and he came into the room in time to pull out her chair for her. "It's an ill wind that blows nobody good," he said in delight. "Now we can catch up on all those questions I wanted to ask you."

Julie shivered. "Somehow, at this point, I don't believe I can ever answer another question again."

He sobered. "Were they tough on you?" he asked. "I don't see what you could be expected to know about our troubles here. What on earth did they ask you?"

"Oh, about Swen Oorth meeting me at the station and what he said about knowing what was going on here, and that he wouldn't tell if it was made worth his while. Not in those words, of course. And about —" She caught herself on the verge of telling him of the whispered conversation she had overheard. Not that it mattered with Hugh, but she had promised not to speak of it.

Hugh laughed. "Come on, mystery girl!"

"— about Lester felling the tree across the road," she finished lamely.

"What could have got into him?" Hugh wondered. "He seemed like a good guy;

hot-headed, of course, but hard-working and popular. I hate to think of what has happened to him.''

''Oh, I don't think he died in the storm,'' Julie reassured him. ''I think —'' she stopped again.

''You don't?'' Hugh was startled. ''Then why are the State Police sitting around here instead of looking for him? We ought to round up all the men we can find and start beating the woods until we lay hands on the fellow.''

Julie shook her head. ''Captain Holt strikes me as a man who knows his own mind and won't welcome suggestions. Anyhow,'' her voice shook, ''can't we forget it for a few minutes?''

''Sorry. I've been thoughtless. We'll forget all about it. Forget everything but us. Tomorrow, if the men don't go back to work, will you try skiing with me? Or do you ski?''

Julie was about to accept with delight when she recalled that she had only one ski suit, the tangerine one which Don did not want her to wear again. She was tempted to explain the reason to Hugh but she had promised.

''I'm no good at it,'' she confessed.

Hugh's face fell; he was so disappointed that she compromised. "But, at least, if the weather stays clear, we can go for a walk."

He brightened. "Fine, I'll hold you to that. Now I'm beginning to get back my confidence," he admitted. "This afternoon when Bruce stood beside me when I was trying to get acquainted with you I thought sure he was planning to cut me out." He added, "I was just about ready to risk my job to have a showdown about it."

"Good heavens," Julie exclaimed in alarm, "you mustn't quarrel with your manager about me. Anyhow, Mr. Bruce isn't interested, in case you care."

"He's interested, all right," Hugh told her. "His whole expression is different when he looks at you. He's prepared to fight for you. But so am I. For I do care. I think you're the first girl I've ever really cared about. I didn't know there were any girls like you. And I want you to like me. I want terribly to have you like me, Julie."

Seeing the expression in his eyes, Julie checked him quickly. "Hugh," she said, "you are being much too serious. We've only known each other a couple of days.

You mustn't —"

" 'Who ever lov'd, that lov'd not at first sight?' " he quoted. "Why mustn't I, Julie? Because I'm too young or too unimportant or too poor?"

There was such deep hurt in his tone that Julie said gently, "It's just that we don't know each other well enough."

His eyes brightened. "Then I do have a chance? Please, Julie, tell me that I have a chance. With any hope at all, I could conquer worlds for you."

"Heavens," she laughed, trying to lighten his intensity, "I wouldn't know what to do with them if you gave them to me."

"You aren't engaged, are you?"

"No," she said, "I'm not engaged."

"That's enough for me," he declared. He looked up as Don called, "Oh, Gordon!" — apologized to Julie, and went over, at Don's gesture, to draw up a fourth chair at the manager's table.

Clarisse, who had been watching the absorbed conversation at Julie's table, called maliciously, "You seem to have bad luck with your boy friends."

"Cut it short, Clarisse," Curtis snarled. At the sound of his angry voice

Captain Holt glanced quickly at him. "You haven't done so well yourself." There was a little pause and then Curtis went on, too enraged with his wife to keep up his pretense of marital happiness. "What were you doing at the smithy yesterday afternoon?"

"The smithy?" Clarisse caught her breath. Julie heard a gasp and saw Florence put down her fork, the color fading from her face. Charlie Keane's eyes were boring into his wife's face.

Julie had a fleeting impression of the abandoned blacksmith shop down by the pond, which she had passed while she was skiing. It was an old log house, the roof fringed with icicles, the two windows staring at her like haunted eyes, a loose board in a shutter rattling eerily. But why did the reference to that gruesome haunted building bring the color to Clarisse's face, drive it from Florence's face? What was the secret shared by the two women?

Don was murmuring to Hugh Gordon who nodded and went out of the dining room. In a few moments Mrs. Blaine gave the signal and chairs were pushed back from the tables. They drifted into the gameroom.

Clarisse glanced at Don who was still talking to Captain Holt, shrugged and turned to Charlie Keane. "Come on, darling," she said gaily, "I'll beat you at gin rummy."

"Just try it," he laughed as he pulled out a chair for her.

"Charlie," Florence said unexpectedly, the effort bringing color back to her face, "I thought we were going to go over our accounts tonight."

"Your businessman always handles yours," he said, "and I can take care of my own, thanks."

His wife turned and went to stand in front of the fireplace, a lovely, frozen woman.

Why, Julie wondered impatiently, was Don talking to Captain Holt instead of keeping an eye on Carrie? Surely he could not have realized how dangerous her position was. She drifted casually toward the door, saw Carrie hurriedly removing dishes from the dining room. She was in a rush. She'd be gone before Don did anything about it.

After a moment's hesitation, Julie went softly up the stairs, pulled on heavy galoshes and buckled them, put on her coat, tied a wool scarf over her hair, took fur-lined mittens, a flashlight. Went noise-lessly down and opened the front door without a sound, closing it behind her.

She circled the house and looked in the windows of the lighted kitchen. Carrie's apron had been tossed over a chair. The towel that had been tied around her jaw lay on the floor where she had dropped it in her haste. She had already gone!

Julie clenched her hands and took a long breath. There wasn't a moment to lose. By the time she could run back for the men and they could get into outdoor cloth-ing, Carrie would be beyond their reach. She'd have to go herself. Then she re-membered the promise she had made to her aunt and whistled softly for Monty. There was no friendly rush, no answering bark, no eager wriggling body anxious to accompany her.

For a moment she hesitated and then she lifted her head, listening intently. In the distance she heard Monty's bark. Bark? He was howling! Howling as he had done when he discovered Swen Oorth's dead body. She was too late. Something had already happened to Car-rie.

Julie began to run, her flashlight wobbling in her hand from excitement and fear. Why, oh why, hadn't she kept Carrie in sight every minute? Why had she taken for granted that Don would inform Captain Holt and that all would be well? She should have realized that with Aunt Deb sitting at the table with them he would not discuss Carrie's danger for fear of her aunt's heart. What a fool she had been!

Something weird, dark in shape, loomed up and Julie's heart was in her throat. What was it? An animal? A man? She let out her breath in a sob of relief. It was only a clump of bushes. She stumbled, skidded over icy snow, pitched into snow banks, pulled herself out again, caught at the trunk of a tree to save herself from pitching into a gully, almost on the edge of the slope where she had skied with such disastrous results.

The barking was louder now. Monty was in a frenzy. There was a rush, the dog was leaping at her, barking its heart out, catching her coat in its teeth, tugging.

"All right, old boy, all right," Julie said. She put her hand on the dog's head. "I'm coming with you. Keep still."

The dog led her through the snow to

228

where there was a frozen log. A log? There was a red stocking cap, a brown wool coat, feet in galoshes. Julie knelt in the snow, touched the bundle that lay there, turned it over. It was Carrie!

Too late. She had come too late. She pulled off her mittens and groped for Carrie's wrist, bent over, heard faint uneven breathing. Carrie was still alive! Julie sagged with relief and then cupped her hands around her mouth and shouted at the top of her voice, "Help! Help!"

The words echoed back from the hillside and suddenly Julie realized that she was in danger. Lester had struck Carrie down, just as she had feared, and now she had revealed where she was. Carrie had been out of the house only a few moments so her attacker could not be far away.

As a belated precaution she switched out the flashlight, crouching close to Carrie. In the darkness she remembered the scene as her flashlight had first caught it. The woman lying like a log in the snow. The trampled ground as though there had been a struggle. And beyond that a trackless waste.

To her groping hand Carrie's face seemed to be growing colder. Julie realized that she could not consider her own personal safety. Carrie must have care and warmth and she could never get her back to the lodge alone. She shouted again and defiantly turned on the flashlight, swung it in wide arcs. Her whole body was stiff with tension and fear, expecting at any moment a blow would strike her down as it had Carrie.

Then there was an answering shout and someone was running toward her.

''Julie!'' Don caught her in his arms. ''What is it? What frightened you? What are you doing here alone? Thank God, you are safe! I lived a century trying to get to you, imagining all sorts of horrors.'' He bent over and his lips brushed her cheek, found her mouth, crushed it with his own. For a moment Julie's hands went out, she clung to him, her lips answered his and then she burrowed her face in his coat.

At last she drew away. ''I'm not alone. It's Carrie. Lester knocked her out. I don't know how badly she is hurt but she is still living.''

The flashlight swung down and Don, with an exclamation, dropped to his knees beside the unconscious woman. Gently he lifted her head, his fingers probing lightly.

''There's a knot the size of a golf ball,'' he said. ''It's a wonder to me she is still alive. I hope to God her skull isn't fractured.'' His voice became a growl, with the deadly note Julie had heard in it once before. ''So they are making war on women now.''

Men were racing up the trail toward them, Charlie Keane far in the lead, Captain Holt and Hugh Gordon side by side, Curtis Wheeler lagging far behind. He was heavier than the other men and he was breathing heavily.

Charlie Keane was hardly out of breath at all. He glanced quickly at Carrie, to ascertain her identity, and then looked around. ''Lester?'' he asked.

''I don't know,'' Don said shortly. At his orders, Charlie Keane and Hugh Gordon lifted the injured woman carefully lest there be any back injury and carried her slowly back to the house. The captain was searching in the snow. There were footprints everywhere, signs of a scuffle.

''Well,'' he said at last oddly. ''Well!''

''What is it?'' Don asked.

Don swung the lantern slowly around,

saw the trampled footprints coming from the house, the scuffed snow, the spot where Carrie had lain, the smooth snow beyond.

"Notice anything?" Holt asked.

"So that's it!" Don exclaimed.

Julie stared at the two men in bewilderment, unable to see what was so apparent, so startling to them. Then she gave an exclamation of her own.

"The basket is gone," she told them. "The basket of food Carrie was taking to Lester. He must have taken it with him."

"It won't be too far away," Captain Holt said, still speaking in that queer manner. "I think we might as well go back. Now, Miss Ames," he went on coldly and she wondered why she had ever thought he was friendly, "perhaps you will be good enough to explain why, after the warning I gave you this afternoon, you came out alone in the dark."

Julie felt like a child who has been scolded. "I was foolish," she admitted. "I realized that while I was waiting for you to come. I wanted to hide in the dark but I couldn't take the chance — for Carrie. All the time I was swinging that flashlight I was ex-expecting to be c-conked

232

on the head. But I'd told Don and he didn't seem to be d-doing anything about C-carrie so I c-came myself.''

The two men exchanged looks but made no comment.

''I whistled for Monty and then I heard him howling. Is she — badly hurt?''

''She'll be lucky to escape a fractured skull,'' Captain Holt said grimly. ''That blow was for keeps. At the best, she probably has a concussion. We'll get the doctor up in the morning. We can't risk moving her into town tonight by car. Her back may be injured.''

They were at the door of the house now and Hugh and Charlie Keane were coming down the stairs. Curtis Wheeler was waiting at the office door for news.

''We put her on her bed,'' Hugh reported, ''and Mrs. Blaine and Clarisse are undressing her.'' He turned to Julie. ''Your aunt is just about frantic about you. You'd better let her know you are all right.''

Julie sent him a reassuring smile and went upstairs. As she passed the Keane room she heard Flo walking up and down, sobbing as though her heart were breaking. Instinctively her hand went out to the doorknob and then she let it drop. She could not intrude on such grief as that.

She tapped softly on Carrie's door and Clarisse opened it a crack, peered out and then stood aside to let her in. "This place is a madhouse," she whispered, her face haggard. "Who's going to be next?"

Julie went to the bed where her aunt was pulling the covers over Carrie. She was still unconscious and breathing noisily. Mrs. Blaine's exhausted face lighted a little as she saw Julie and she stretched out one slender hand to touch the girl as though to reassure herself that her niece was really safe and sound.

"You go to your own room and go to bed, Aunt Deb," Julie said. "You need rest. I'll sit up with Carrie tonight."

Her aunt nodded wearily. "I think I will. I'm so sorry to have involved you in this nightmare, Julie."

Clarisse went out with Mrs. Blaine, who said: "Lock the door, dear. Don't let anyone in."

Julie nodded, locked the door and went back to sit beside the bed where Carrie, her poor scarred face no longer concealed, lay unconscious, moaning now and then.

She found an extra blanket lying over a chair, tucked it around her and settled down for her vigil. But she was not thinking of the latest disaster at the Blaine hunting lodge. She was thinking of Don's arms tight around her, Don's voice wild with anxiety about her, Don's lips on hers.

I won't sleep tonight, she told herself. I feel as though I'd never sleep again. Her long lashes touched her cheeks. She opened her eyes, held them open by sheer will power. They closed again. She was young and healthy and she had had little sleep the night before. Her breathing became slow and even. She slept.

Outside the door a floorboard creaked, something moved. She slept on.

ii

It was broad daylight when Julie was awakened by the sound of the injured woman stirring in the bed. She was instantly alert. Carrie's eyes fluttered open, gazed at her in perplexity and closed again without recognition. Julie got out of the chair and stretched her cramped body. She unlocked the door and nearly sprawled over Don, who slept in a chair across the doorway.

He looked very young, his hair tousled, his mouth, usually so stern, boyish and defenseless. Abruptly he opened his eyes. He grinned and got up.

''Were you there all night?'' Julie asked in a whisper.

''I didn't want you to be the next one to be hit over the head,'' he said. He grinned. ''A fine watchdog I turned out to be. No thanks to me someone didn't get in. How's Carrie?''

''She opened her eyes once but she didn't recognize me.''

Don picked up the chair and carried it back to his own room. Down the hall another door opened and Mrs. Blaine came out in a dark blue wool dress. She slipped past Julie to look at Carrie.

''I'll stay with her until you've had time to bathe and change.''

Julie went to her own room and stood staring. The dresser drawers were open, clothes lay on the floor. She pulled aside the curtain that hung over the wardrobe. The clothes had been moved and the tangerine ski suit, which she had hidden at

the back under a raincoat, was in the front
where someone had been able to examine
it at leisure.

XIII

TWO HOURS later, to her own incredulous surprise, Julie found herself on a plane beside Don Bruce, flying to New York. She pulled off her small hat, shook loose the soft waves of her black hair, and leaned back in her seat.

"I can't believe I'm here and I still don't know why."

Don had bent over her to unfasten her seat belt. He smiled reassuringly. "When you came down and told us someone had found that tangerine ski suit, Captain Holt and I knew something had to be done — fast. He had planned to get the sergeant back today to guard you, but Carrie's accident will delay matters. The State Police are shorthanded. The sergeant's job is escorting Carrie to the hospital before further attacks can be made on her. I appointed myself your deputy guard, and as I have to go to New York, we thought it was best for you to go along.''

He glanced down at her stormy face. ''Your aunt agreed with me that it was for the best.''

''You needn't think I'll stay in New York,'' Julie said resolutely. ''I intend to see this thing through with Aunt Deb and —''

''All right! All right!'' Don capitulated with a laugh. ''By tomorrow, Holt will have the sergeant on hand. But,'' he took a long breath, ''today is mine. And I intend to make the most of it. That is — I'll be busy all day but tonight we can dine and dance somewhere.'' As she hesitated, he pleaded, ''Please, Julie.''

She met his ardent gaze almost shyly. ''I'd love to,'' she declared.

Something flared up in his eyes. Not yet, she thought in a panic. Not yet. To forestall his eager speech she said gaily, ''You've explained why I am being kidnapped but not why you are going to New York.''

Don hesitated and she said quickly, ''I'm sorry. I shouldn't have asked. I knew you had some secret —''

"What do you mean by that?" he asked sharply.

Color flooded her cheeks at his tone. "Well, I — anyone could have seen that you and Captain Holt had met before, though you pretended to be strangers — and that he trusted you, and that there was something . . ." Her voice trailed off.

"Go on," he said grimly, "what else have you noticed?"

"The way you watch the superintendents," Julie told him frankly. "As though you kept waiting for something to happen."

"Well, what a detective I've turned out to be," Don said in disgust.

"Is that what you are — a detective?"

"Not exactly. Someday I'll tell you all about it. Someday, Julie, I'll tell you all there is to know about Don Bruce, if you care to know it. But —"

"I understand. I won't ask any questions. Except when do we go back?"

"*I* go back in the morning. Tomorrow I'm going to try to talk the men into returning to work. But you —"

"I'm going, too," she said. "Try to stop me."

Half an hour later, during which both

240

had been absorbed in their thoughts, Julie asked abruptly, ''Don, do you think you can do it?''

He came back from a long private journey. ''Do what?''

''Persuade the men to go back to work.''

''I don't know,'' he said slowly. ''They are good men who are being stirred up by someone. I think they'd work if they were sure Lester would get a fair break.''

''Lester!'' Julie sat bolt upright, her eyes snapping. ''After the way he struck down Carrie when she was trying to help him?'' Unexpectedly she clutched at his arm. ''Don, what was so queer about the snow last night when we found her? What did you and Captain Holt see that I missed?''

Don grinned, ''Ah, my gimlet-eyed sleuth! So there is something you missed.'' He sobered. ''You won't panic?''

''Of course not.''

''Well,'' he said slowly, ''there were footprints, lots of them, leading up to where Carrie fell. But none that led away from her into the woods.''

Julie looked at him, frowning, while

she puzzled it out. "You mean," she said at last, her voice almost a whisper, "it wasn't Lester who struck her. It was someone who came back to the lodge. One of us."

"One of us," Don said steadily. His hand closed over hers. "It almost had to be that way. And we're bound to find out which one it is. Don't look so little and white and scared, Julie."

After a moment he added, "You've been an enormous help, you know, though you took a risk I can hardly forgive you for."

"A help?"

He nodded. "If you hadn't followed almost on Carrie's heels, the person who attacked her would undoubtedly have had time to make misleading tracks off into the woods. But when you appeared, there was no time. He — or she — dared not risk being late in putting in an appearance at the lodge or among the rest of us. Obviously he waited behind a tree until we came up, and joined us. The ground leading to Carrie was all trampled. So that trackless waste pointed right back to the lodge and the camp."

Julie sat thinking about what she had

heard, unaware of the flight. Almost before she knew it, Don was fastening her seat belt and the plane came smoothly down on the runway at La Guardia airport. Don hailed a taxi and drove her to Manhattan. It was a clear cold day with a strong wind blowing but there was no trace of snow. The roar of traffic, the impact of sound — riveting machines, motors, footsteps, voices, traffic on the ground and above the ground and under the ground — seemed deafening after the deep silence of the Maine woods.

Don made dinner arrangements and left her with a wave of the hand.

"Where to, Miss?" the driver asked and Julie realized that she had been watching that tall, lithe figure striding purposefully away through the crowds in front of Grand Central Station.

"I don't know. You might as well leave me here." She opened her handbag.

"Your friend paid me. Plenty," the driver said.

Julie stood hesitating, unaware of the hurrying people who bumped into her, unaware that many of them paused for a second look at her, cheeks pink with the sting of the wind, eyes shining, face warmed and made radiant by the immemorial look of the woman in love.

She lunched at the Colony, waving to acquaintances at several tables but refusing to join them. If she did, they were bound to discuss her wedding plans, as no public announcement had been made of breaking her engagement. She did not want to lie about it, nor did she want to explain that she had changed her mind. It was simpler to sit alone. But the awkward position in which she found herself made it clear that she could not continue to drift along. Something definite and final must be done about Quentin.

In the afternoon she went shopping for an evening dress. She was difficult to please. For some reason which she did not analyze to herself it seemed vitally important to look her best tonight. She sat watching slim models parade before her, walking with their long graceful step, turning, swaying, a mechanical smile on their lips.

At length a slender girl modeled a dress of coral crepe that left her shoulders bare and fell in swirling folds to her feet.

"This model," the saleswoman said, "is called 'Spring Dawn.'"

"I'll try it," Julie decided. The saleswoman slipped the gown over her head, the color brought out the delicate glow of her skin, made her hair seem darker, her eyes deeper.

The saleswoman took a long breath. "It was made for madam."

When the dress had been purchased it was only four o'clock. There were still three hours to fill before it would be time to dress for dinner. Julie remembered the announcement of an art exhibit that she had planned to see, called a taxi, and then surprised herself by giving the address of Newton Brewster's Fifth Avenue townhouse instead of the gallery on Fifty-seventh Street.

Central Park was bleak as she passed it. The Brewster house, a narrow four-story building with a white marble façade, was near the Metropolitan Museum of Art. Julie went up a flight of marble steps and rang the bell. The door was opened promptly by Stamm, the elderly butler who had headed Brewster's domestic staff for thirty years.

"Miss Ames," he said, a welcoming smile on his customarily blank face.

"Is Mr. Brewster in? I hoped he'd offer

me some tea.''

Stamm hesitated. ''He'll be delighted to see you if he is at leisure,'' he said at last. He led her into a long narrow library, with leather-bound books, deep chairs and good reading lamps, and took her fur coat. When he had gone out, Julie strolled to one of the long windows that looked out on the back of the house and the New Yorker's greatest luxury, a miniature garden. The window was slightly open and apparently so was the next one, which opened, as she knew, into Brewster's study.

She heard Brewster's impatient voice. ''What is it, Stamm? I told you I wasn't to be disturbed.''

''It's Miss Ames, sir. She wondered if you would offer her some tea.''

''Have it served in the library in a quarter of an hour,'' Brewster said. ''Now then, Major, is there anything else I can do for you?''

Julie's heart leaped as she heard Don's voice say, '''You've done more for me that I could have accomplished in a month unaided. I'm afraid I've taken up too much of your time.''

''I don't know how I could have used

it more profitably. But won't you join us for tea?''

''Thank you, sir. It will be a great pleasure.''

''By the way,'' Brewster chuckled, ''it might be as well for you to meet Julie under this roof so she can see that I sponsor you. I got a letter from her this morning asking what I know about you and why I had referred to you as a dangerous man.''

''She asked you that?''

As Julie heard the whiplash tone she flung out her hand, as though he could see her, pleading mutely for forgiveness.

''She did, indeed. You must have made quite an impression.''

''A poor impression, apparently,'' Don said again. ''Sorry I can't wait for tea, sir. I have a lot of things to attend to before I go back to Maine in the morning.''

In a few moments Newton Brewster came into the library, both hands outstretched. ''Welcome, my dear! This is treating me like an old friend, indeed.''

While Stamm placed the tea things before Julie, Brewster chatted about her plane trip and the blizzard in Maine.

When the butler had withdrawn and Julie was busying herself with teapot, hot water, lemon and sugar, he said, "Now then, tell me about your Aunt Deb. Is she all right?"

"She is wonderful," Julie said simply.

"The strain of this murder isn't too much for her?" Brewster asked anxiously.

Julie reassured him.

"I suppose you've seen the New York papers."

No, Julie confessed, she hadn't. She'd been too busy.

"They are having a field day with Oorth's murder at your aunt's lodge. The Blaines are always news and when you get society mixed up in murder, the papers really spread themselves. What's your opinion of this business, my dear?"

"I don't know," Julie admitted. "At first, I thought Lester was the criminal." She did not attempt to explain who Lester was. She realized that Don had discussed the whole case with the older man. But who *was* Don? What was he? Why had Mr. Brewster called him Major? When would the mystery concerning him be cleared up?

"Then," she went on, "I thought it was one of the two women. But neither of them would have any reason for hurting Carrie. So I just don't know."

There was a twinkle in Brewster's eyes, a hint of amusement in his voice as he said, "I gather you have been harboring some suspicions about the new manager, Don Bruce."

"You're the one who told me he was dangerous," she retorted.

Brewster chuckled outright. "Are you sure you haven't found him so?"

Julie could feel her face flame. Darn, she thought, I wish there weren't such a thing as a blush. She said aloud, "Who is he, Mr. Brewster?"

"I trust you a great deal, my dear, or I wouldn't answer that question. But, I think, under the circumstances —"

"What circumstances?"

"I suspect," he said, with a searching look at her, "that it is as important for you to believe in Bruce as it is for him to have your faith. Don Bruce is one of the most daring as well as most level-headed men I know. He's a kind of trouble shooter for Uncle Sam. You remember the Texas story about the town that had a riot?

249

The citizens sent for help. Along came a single Texas Ranger. 'Only one Ranger?' they protested. 'Wal-l' he drawled, 'there's only one riot.' When there's only one riot they send Major Bruce.''

ii

When Julie had slipped the coral crepe evening dress over her head in the hotel room she smiled in approval at the girl in the mirror. Then she opened the box which a messenger had delivered a short time before and gave a cry of delight. She pinned on the white orchid and read the card: ''This evening belongs to me — remember? Don.'' She wondered whether he had forgiven her for asking Mr. Brewster about him or whether the orchid had been ordered before he had gone to the Fifth Avenue house.

She had never before seen Don in dinner clothes. As he came toward her she saw that other women watched the way he moved and the carriage of his head.

His eyes swept over her, noticed the orchid, passed on without comment. He took her evening cape from her and put

250

it over her shoulders. Julie's question was answered. He had not forgiven her.

"Thank you for the orchid," she said. "It's lovely."

"So are you," he replied, but his tone was cool, that of an attentive escort, nothing more.

The roof restaurant at which he had reserved a table was one where she had often gone with Quentin. When the waiter had pulled out her chair Julie looked around. At her low exclamation of consternation Don was instantly alert, the cool aloofness gone from his face.

"What is it?" he asked.

"There's Quentin. My — the man I was engaged to marry. When he sees me in New York, after thinking I am in Maine, and dining and dancing with another man — Oh, dear," she wailed.

Don laughed softly. "So far," he reminded her, "you haven't danced with me. Come on. And don't worry about Quentin. I'll handle him."

As they moved across the dance floor Julie looked up. To her relief Don was smiling down at her. "I knew you'd dance like this," he said. "It seems to me we've been dancing together all our lives."

The music of the name band throbbed softly. Beside them and around them other couples moved to the rhythm, talked and laughed. At small candle-lit tables waiters lifted covers from hot dishes. Outside the windows was spread the brilliant panorama of New York, the long span of the bridges, the lights of Long Island on the east, of New Jersey on the west, and darkling between them the black flood of the rivers.

Julie moved as though she were floating through a dream, with Don's arms around her, Don's hand guiding her through intricate steps. The music stopped at last and he released her, met her eyes, his own glowing.

"Julie," he began.

"Julie!" The word was almost a shout.

Quentin Harrington had pushed back his chair from the table beside the dance floor and he was glowering at her. Julie was aware that the other members of his party were watching them with surprised amusement.

"He-hello, Quentin," she stammered.

"What on earth are you doing here? I just got a letter from you this morning from Maine. Why didn't you tell me you were coming? And what's all this about a murder? 'Julie Ames, last season's sensational debutante, is among the guests at Mrs. James Blaine's lodge where the crime occurred. Miss Ames, whose marriage to Quentin Harrington is expected to be one of the events of the spring season' — blah, blah, blah — how do you think I liked getting that along with my morning coffee?''

If Quentin had had any knowledge of women he would never have treated the murder as an event more disturbing to him than it had been to her. He rushed on to his doom. He looked at her partner and recognized the laughing buccaneer from the restaurant beside the skating rink.

''Where on earth did you meet that fellow?'' he exploded, filled with jealousy.

Julie's color rose. ''You seem to have mislaid your manners, Quentin,'' she said crisply. ''You are making a scene and attracting attention. When you have apologized I will introduce you.''

''Apologized! I have a right to be annoyed when you behave this way.''

''Anyone would think,'' Julie sputtered furiously, ''that I got involved in murder just to annoy you.''

"Just a minute," Don interposed levelly. "Miss Ames's behavior is not to be made the subject of public discussion. If you care to come to our table you can do so, as long as you aren't offensive."

Quentin's face seemed to swell with rage but under Don's icy tone, his level eyes, something in his manner of a man accustomed to giving commands, he capitulated quietly enough.

Don pulled out Julie's chair, motioned the waiter to bring another one for Quentin. The latter refused it.

"What I have to say to Julie I don't intend to say before a third person."

"Then I'm afraid," Don said, "you'll have to wait for another occasion. This is my evening."

"You don't seem to realize," Quentin said, "that Julie is engaged to me."

"I *was* engaged to you," Julie corrected him. "I gave back your ring because you tried to dominate my whole life."

"Someone has to, if you go away for a couple of days, get involved in murder and turn up with this — this buccaneer."

"You are being insulting, Quentin."

"I won't be made a fool of. You've got

to choose. Who is this man?''

''His name is Don Bruce,'' Julie said.

''And what is he to you?''

''If the Bruce luck holds,'' Don intervened silkily, ''I'm the man who is going to marry Julie. Now I suggest you return to your own party, Harrington. This evening, as I told you before, belongs to me. Dance, Julie?''

He swept her out on the floor, away from the glowering Quentin, looked down at her face and laughed softly.

''You look as though the sky had fallen in on you.''

''I expect it to fall on you,'' Julie retorted. ''When you made that speech to Quentin about — about the Bruce luck, I thought a thunderbolt would strike you. Poor Quentin!''

''Quentin deserves a lesson,'' Don told her.

''Of course he does,'' she admitted, ''but if I know him, I'm the one who will be punished.''

''What do you mean?''

''He'll never give up so easily. He'll get in touch with Aunt Deb and warn her that I was out dancing with — a buccaneer.'' She began to laugh helplessly.

"That you are going to marry a buccaneer," Don corrected her.

"Good heavens, he wouldn't tell her that!" Julie said in consternation. "What can we do about it?"

"You'll have to stay here," Don decided. "It's the only way you can prove to Quentin that we aren't really engaged."

"And leave Aunt Deb alone there with a — a murderer? I'm going back with you and nothing can stop me."

"Then," Don said cooly, "I'm afraid you have no choice. If you go back, you go as my affianced wife."

XIV

IT WAS EARLY afternoon when the taxi from the airport deposited Julie and Don in front of the general store. Less than a week ago Julie had reached the village and been met by Swen Oorth on what proved to be the last day of his life. That day there had been a heavy snowstorm.

Today, the shining black road had been cleared of snow and ice by the mill plows. The sun gilded treetops. The air was bracing. The sky was wearing a turquoise blue print with a design of white cirrus feathers. Blue jays planed through the dark green branches of a towering hemlock to the accompaniment of raucous squawks.

Julie was surprised that Don had dismissed the taxi in a village so disinclined to do any favors for guests from the Blaine hunting lodge or loggers at the camp.

257

Then she saw what his quick eyes had seen first. Aunt Deb's estate wagon was parked in front of the general store. There would be no difficulty about getting home.

Don lifted Julie's luggage into the back of the car and looked around. "I wonder who drove it in?" He looked around him, frowning. "Julie," he said abruptly, "wait in the store for me, will you? It's too cold for you out of doors. I won't be long."

"Where are you going?"

The sternness in his face vanished as he smiled down at her. "Your eyes are big as saucers. I'm just going to take a look around. There seems to be an unusual amount of activity taking place in the village."

"Let me go with you," Julie begged.

He looked at her doubtfully and then tucked her hand under his arm. "All right," he capitulated, "come along but be sure to let me know when you get cold."

The village, as Don had observed, was buzzing with activity, thronged with automobiles of all vintages, from ancient Fords to this year's Lincolns, with a few battered pickup trucks and a couple of long rakish foreign sports cars. There were more people than usual on the sidewalks, gathered in little groups, talking and arguing. The largest and most vociferous of these groups was outside the post office.

Julie noticed in surprise that Hugh Gordon was the center of this group. As they approached it, Don's hand closed over hers. She looked up at his face and found it alert. He seemed to be braced for action.

"Trouble brewing," he told her softly.

"Time we ran them all out of Maine," one of the men shouted.

"You can't deprive a lot of men of their jobs," Hugh pointed out reasonably. "Just because of one single individual. They are good guys. I know them. They work hard for the money they get. There's no sense in punishing them. They haven't harmed anyone. Lester was the troublemaker. He's the one you are after."

Hugh caught sight of Julie and Don and shouldered his way through the hostile crowd toward them. "Whew!" he said, mopping his head. "Am I glad to see you! I was afraid for a while that I had a near riot on my hands. These people are all worked up.''

''And why not?'' called a woman shrilly. ''Downing was my own husband's second cousin. As nice a man as you'd want to know. Someone at Blaine's killed him and they covered it up. Called it a hunting accident. And then Swen Oorth was shot the same way. My sister-in-law's uncle knows a man on the State Police, and he said Oorth died just like Downing did. And now it's Carrie, poor soul, who set a lot of store by Mrs. Blaine and offered to help out when no one else would. And someone tried to murder her. It's got to stop!''

''It will stop!'' Don's voice rang out strong and clear. ''We're not covering up a thing. The State Police won't quit until they've got the guilty person.'' His angry eyes moved from face to face. ''But if you people want justice, try to be just. You're acting like a mob right now. We're not going to condemn anyone, not even Lester, until he's had a fair hearing. Get that straight.''

''Where is he?'' shouted a voice.

''I don't know,'' Don admitted. ''But I do know this. He wasn't driven away, as the loggers seem to think. He went of his own free will. I'm convinced that he is alive and hiding. But'' — as there was a mutter, he raised his hand — ''but,'' he said louder, his voice dominating the turmoil, ''flight does not necessarily mean guilt. It may be that he was afraid. This country was based on law, on trial by jury, and that's what Lester will have when we find him — and we will find him — if there is evidence to justify his arrest.''

There was furtive movement in the crowd and a mutter of, ''String him up.''

''Mob violence,'' Don said, his voice ringing, ''trial by public opinion, accusations without proof — these are ugly, cowardly and treacherous — yes, treacherous — methods of dealing with a man. Lester is going to have justice under law. Fair play. Is that clear?''

Apparently it was. One by one they drifted away, ashamed. Don turned to Hugh.

''Did you drive the estate wagon?''

Hugh nodded.

''Will you take Julie up to the lodge? I'll get a lift later on.'' Don touched a finger to his hat in salute and went quickly down the village street.

Hugh helped Julie into the car and

turned on the heater. He sat at the wheel in no hurry to move, and as the hot air filled the car Julie flung open her coat.

"This is a gift straight from heaven, Julie," he said. "I didn't think I'd ever have another chance to talk to you."

"Why on earth not?" she exclaimed in surprise.

"Mrs. Blaine got a telegram last night announcing that you were engaged to marry Mr. Bruce."

"Good heavens! Quentin certainly didn't waste any time."

"I suppose," Hugh said, "I should have expected it. A girl like you. I don't know what got into me, thinking I might have a chance with you. Only, you see," he added simply, his voice unsteady, "I fell in love with you. I couldn't help it. You were what I didn't know even existed."

Julie felt his pain and longed to ease it, to explain to him that she was not the one who had sent her Aunt Deb that telegram announcing her engagement. But, she realized, it would make no real difference. Whether or not she married Don, and he had never asked her, she knew that she loved him with all her heart, that she could never marry anyone else.

"I'm terribly sorry," she began.

"No reason why you'd ever look at me," he said drearily. "I have nothing to offer you. No money, no position, nothing."

"But that's ridiculous," Julie told him. "Those aren't the things that matter. They have nothing whatever to do with it. You must believe me, Hugh. And anyhow, you've got a lot. You're very attractive. That nonsense about money and position —"

"Do you think they don't count?" he asked bitterly.

"With some people, of course," she admitted. "There are always people to whom money matters most — frightened people. And it wasn't —" She broke off. She'd been about to say she wasn't engaged to Don Bruce because of money and position; then she remembered that she wasn't really engaged to him at all.

Hugh turned suddenly and put his hand on hers, his eyes pleading. "Julie, what could I do to make you love me?"

She shook her head, trying to speak lightly, not to hurt him more than she could help because he seemed so sensitive to being hurt. "I'm just not the right girl for you, Hugh."

"You mean I'm not the right man for you. And the Boss is." His hand tightened on the wheel and he stared unseeingly through the windshield. He took a long breath and then turned to smile at her. "You know," he said gaily, "you look like an oriole in that yellow sports suit."

He started the car, moved out of the parking space, turned toward the road that led to the lumber camp. Julie took a quick look around but there was no sign of Don.

"You people arrived in the nick of time," Hugh said cheerfully. "Those hot-headed citizens were on the verge of treating me rough because of the trouble up at the camp. That was quite a speech the Boss made to that mob. Sent them away with their tails between their legs. He certainly knew how to handle them. I guess he's had a lot of experience managing men. What was his job before the war?"

"I don't know," Julie admitted. "Look, that's where the tree dropped across the road and nearly killed me." She shuddered. "Why did Lester do it?"

"He never meant to hurt you, Julie," Hugh declared. "He couldn't even have known you were coming. I don't see how any of the loggers could have known that you were coming. But I do think Lester meant to kill Oorth and when that failed he tried again at the cabin and then got scared and ran out into the blizzard and froze to death. So why Bruce wanted people to think he is still alive —''

''Because he really believes that Lester is alive,'' Julie said.

''Alive! Then he's the one who attacked poor Carrie.''

Julie, remembering the foot prints that had stopped, shivered. Which one, she thought; which one was it? All of a sudden it was urgently important to know.

''How is Carrie?'' she asked.

''Lucky, according to the doctor. She had a bad concussion. She's conscious part of the time but she's in pain and has a headache and can't focus her eyes very well. The doctor said she must not be moved, that she couldn't stand a fifty-mile trip to the hospital. But she doesn't remember what happened to her.''

At the lodge Hugh got out to open the door for her. As she stepped from the car he put his hand on her arm. ''Julie,'' he said impulsively, ''be careful. Please be careful. If the Boss is right and Lester is still alive, evil is loose here.''

Julie smiled at him tremulously. ''Thanks, Hugh. I'll be careful.'' She opened the door of the lodge and went into the warm house.

Mrs. Blaine hastened down the stairs to meet her. ''My dear,'' she exclaimed, ''I had the most extraordinary telegram from Quentin last night. What is it all about?''

Julie glanced around, saw Florence Keane in the gameroom and said, ''I'll tell you later. But there's nothing for you to worry about. Nothing at all. Except yourself. You are much too tired, Aunt Deb.''

She was alarmed by her aunt's pallor, the deep purple shadows under her eyes.

''It's just the strain and the excitement,'' her aunt said. ''Florence has been splendid. She sat up with Carrie all night and she has helped me with the cooking.''

Hearing her name, Florence strolled out into the hall. ''It's good to have work to do, to feel useful for once in my life. I'm half sorry that Captain Holt has taken my job away.''

Mrs. Blaine explained to her niece that

the captain had arranged for a nurse to look after Carrie and had provided a couple to take over the housework. The kitchen door opened and Julie caught sight of the new houseman. Judging by the breadth of his shoulders and his military carriage, Captain Holt had provided a man from his own staff. He was taking no more chances.

Florence held out a slim hand, glittering with rings, to Julie. "I was so glad to hear of your engagement. Mr. Bruce is an unusual person. I congratulate you and wish you every happiness."

Don came into the house. He spoke before Julie could frame a reply. "I'm the one who gets the congratulations," he said with a warning glance at Julie. "But I was born with the Bruce luck."

ii

Don climbed up on the stump of a tree and looked at the loggers who had assembled. What am I going to say to them, he wondered. How am I going to bring them back to their senses? If I say the wrong thing, strike the wrong note, they won't listen to me. And yet this battle — and it's being fought all over the world today — has to be won.

The battle for men's minds. The strange new warfare and yet a kind for which there were no tested rules, no convenient manuals to follow as there were in training men's bodies. All that could be done was to explain as clearly, as honestly as he knew how and trust to making an appeal to the best in the other fellow's nature.

The enemy used the opposite tactics. He appealed to the worst in a man, to his weakness and envy and hatred and self-pity; to his grudge against others and against life itself; to his fears.

How could you answer that? Would they listen if you said, "What we offer you is the right to stand on your own feet, to hew out your own future, to speak your own mind, to walk through the world proud and unafraid. We offer you the burden of being responsible for your own actions; we offer you the chance to be men — not just free men but whole men. We offer you the opportunity for which generations of men have struggled and suffered. It's all yours but each of you must earn it for himself."

Don's eyes moved slowly from face to face until he had collected their attention. When he began to speak it was in an easy, conversational tone.

"I asked you to meet me here," he said, "because it's high time we talked things over, got our opinions out into the light of day where we can look at them. That's the American way and it's a good way."

Somewhere a man gave a jeering laugh. Don disregarded it and went on, unhurried.

"You know what the situation was here. Mrs. Blaine discovered that unless the timber could be cut and sold by April, she not only would lose her husband's estate but, what mattered even more to her, she would be unable to meet the debts Jim Blaine had incurred by backing loans for worthless friends.

"She employed you at excellent wages and provided fine working conditions."

There was a boo.

"Suppose," Don said sharply, "you tell me where you'd get better conditions or wages. If you've got any facts, let's hear them."

There was a moment of silence and he went on, "Mrs. Blaine also hired, as her superintendents, men who had suffered in the service of their country, except for her manager, Downing, who was a native product and, from all I can make out, a just and fine man.''

''No one said anything against Downing,'' shouted one of the loggers. ''If you know what's good for you, you'll lay off him. Downing was a right guy and he got shot for it.''

Don held up his hand. ''You'll all have to chance to say what you have on your minds. But we've got to take it one at a time.'' When they were quiet he said, ''Some weeks ago Downing was killed.''

This time no one spoke. They seemed to be holding their breath. Don could feel their hostility as though they had reached out with their hands to pull him down.

''It was assumed that his death was the result of a hunting accident.''

There was an outbreak of shouts, boos, hisses. Don waited quietly for it to stop.

''We no longer think that. Since the murder of Swen Oorth I believe, and so do the Police, that Downing was deliberately murdered. We are trying to get at the truth.''

''That's a lie! You're covering up the

truth,'' yelled a man down in front. "You covered it up all along until Oorth died the same way and you couldn't get by with it any longer. Now you'd like to pin the murders on Lester, and we won't let you. We want Lester!"

The other loggers took up the chant. *"We want Lester! We want Lester!"*

That mass chanting was the most dangerous thing Don had to face and he knew it. Once the men began acting and thinking like a mob instead of like individuals he was in for trouble. He drew a deep breath and forced himself to relax. He did not move, standing as motionless, as easily as he had done from the start. His very stillness. served to quiet them as no argument could have done.

"I swear to you," he said when they would listen, "that we are not trying to cover up anything. Lester brought suspicion on himself by his own stupidity in running away. If he will come back, he will be given every opportunity to clear himself. I'll pay for his lawyer out of my own pocket and see that he has a good one. But meantime we are looking for a murderer and we intend to find him."

"Yeah? It looks like it!"

"I said we intend to find him. We do. And we intend to do more than that. We intend to find out who has been deliberately trying to poison your minds against the Blaine outfit — and against the whole American system."

The men were silent, alert.

Don went on, his voice ringing out dramatically and with a sincerity they could not fail to believe. "Now I'm going to tell you something — something I hoped need not be made public for a lot of reasons. And one of those reasons was your own self-respect as human beings."

The men were motionless, as though frozen.

"I'm going to tell you," Don said, "exactly what has been happening here. You've been taken for a ride. You've been made fools of. *And you let it happen*. You've been getting a dose of propaganda. And do you know who paid for it? The Reds! That money came straight out of Communist pockets and into the pocket of some man here. You've been experiencing a first-hand course in brainwashing. How do you like it, boys?"

They looked at him in angry disbelief, changing to doubt, becoming a startled half-credulity.

"Shall I tell you the kind of poison you've been listening to and believing? You've been told that you aren't treated fairly. But in Russia you'd take the job they gave you at the wage they chose to pay and live in a room, or a part of a room they assigned to you.

"You've been told you ought to destroy your government by force and take control. But in satellite countries it's the Russians who take control and the guy who doesn't like it lands in a concentration camp. Ever hear how many millions are in concentration camps today?

"You've been told that qualities like honor and truthfulness and simple honesty are bourgeois virtues, that any contemptible action is justified if you end by getting what you want.

"You've been told that religion is a lot of hooey, that the idea of the family is sentimental nonsense. If you don't like your father or your son, turn them in to the authorities!

"You've been told that the State does not exist to serve man but that man exists to serve the State — meekly, dumbly, like sheep, and no back talk.

"You've been told you aren't smart enough to figure things out for yourselves, that you need a Commissar to do it for you."

Don paused. The men seemed to cower under his tongue-lashing. He stood tall, erect, his eyes flashing, the face of a fighting man aglow with his own emotion. Then he made a gesture with his hands.

"Well, boys, that's my side of it. A fine woman needs your help. She is willing to deal fairly with you. If you have any honest grievance, we will do anything in our power to correct it. But I ask you — every one of you — to ask yourselves one question: Why do you feel the Blaine outfit is persecuting Lester? By your own observation or by the sly innuendoes of someone else?"

He stopped. There was a long silence. The anger dropped from his face. Unexpectedly he grinned. "I've spoken my piece. Now it's your turn." He jumped off the stump, leaned against a tree trunk, waited. The men milled together in small groups, talking, gesticulating, arguing.

It was in their hands now. He had done the best he could. Had he made a mistake to use that phrase "brain-washing?" And yet it had been the truth. How would they react to knowing they had simply been pawns in the game of someone else? Would they ever admit they had been badly fooled?

At length one of the men took Don's place on the stump.

''All right, Mr. Bruce,'' he said, ''you've spoken fairly. We want to do the right thing by Mrs. Blaine and by ourselves. You say a fair investigation is being made of these murders. We're willing to wait and see. You say no one is persecuting Lester. We've been talking among ourselves, trying to get at the right of it. We got to admit we never saw any evidence that Lester wasn't getting a fair deal. He was the one told us the Blaine outfit was against him. We don't know where the truth lies. But until one side is proved to be wrong, the strike is off and we're going to report back to work in the morning.''

Don strode forward and held out his hand. After a moment's hesitation the spokesman for the loggers took it.

''What we can't figure out, Mr. Bruce, is how you know what we were told. You weren't even here at the time and yet you mighta been listening in.''

Don laughed. ''I knew because that's the bait they catch suckers with,'' he said.

The spokesman for the loggers turned a dull red. ''That's hitting below the belt,'' he admitted, ''but after hearing what you've got to say I guess we were suckers at that. Makes a guy feel kinda foolish to know he swallowed all that stuff without even thinking whether it was true or not.''

Don smiled grimly. ''There are a lot of people in the world today who are feeling more than foolish now they've got a good look at what they fell for. For some of them it's too late.''

The spokesman for the loggers shuffled his feet awkwardly. ''Well, one thing sure, it won't be so easy for the next guy who tries it on us.''

''I have one more question,'' Don said. ''Who tried to make you discontented with conditions here? Who told you the Blaine outfit was covering up the murder of Downing?''

''Lester,'' the logger said.

Don blinked in his bewilderment. Lester! In that case, he thought, I've been all wrong about everything. Lester is the wrong man. This is impossible.

"How much did Downing know about the growing discontent among you men?"

The logger ruminated, staring at the snow-covered ground. "That's a funny thing," he admitted at last. "Downing was sure sore at Lester but he had his eye on someone else."

"Who?"

"I don't know. He said he could handle it by himself."

XV

THE note was lying on the rug in her room where it had been slipped under the door. Julie opened it.

> Meet me at the smithy at four o'clock. Key in office. Must talk to you privately. Don't mention this. Vitally important. Love.
>
> DON

Afterwards Julie blushed when she recalled that she had not hesitated for a single moment, that it never occurred to her to ignore a summons from Don, however odd it might appear.

She put on the new ski suit she had bought in New York, though she was aware that she might as well flaunt the tangerine suit now that her ownership of

278

it was established. The new one was dark blue with a heavy ribbed yellow sweater. She pulled a yellow cap down over her dark curls, buckled galoshes and stole downstairs.

The office was empty except for Monty. A large key labeled SMITHY hung from the rack beside the desk. Julie held her breath and listened before easing the key gently off its hook and dropping it into the pocket of her jacket. Monty waged his tail and gazed at her with expectant brown eyes. As she started out his head tilted slightly, his tail was motionless, his eyes reproachful. She shook her head. He whined.

Julie looked at the tall clock in the hall before she let herself out. Twenty minutes of four. She could easily reach the smithy and return before her aunt became anxious about her. Then she remembered her promise and let the ecstatic Monty accompany her.

As she turned into the pond road she thought she saw a shadow, like an uneasy ghost, flit from tree to tree in the heavy timber. For several minutes she had had a prickly sense that she was not alone.

She stopped. Listened. Should she go

back? She looked up at the brilliant blue sky, at the gold-tipped tops of trees where the sun was gilding them, heard the purr of an automobile motor on the road she had left, the ring of skates on the ice beyond. Silly. What could happen so near civilization? And yet the winter days were short. Twilight would fall soon. It would be very dark.

"Imagination is my fortune, kind sir, she said," she hummed under her breath and went on. She felt like singing. However much Don's note might surprise her, she remembered he had signed it with love. When he had told her that if she returned to Maine it must be as his affianced wife, there had been so much laughter in his eyes that she had assumed he was not serious. But suppose — after all, Newton Brewster, who was a sound psychologist, believed that Don cared for her. What had he said? That Don needed her faith in him.

Julie tried to step lightly across the stretch of snow that separated the log building from the pond road. But her feet went *cr-runch! cr-runch!* The sun had reached the room of the smithy, and each icicle pendant from the overhand

280

appeared to drip flame. The two windows made her think shiveringly of eyes with no soul behind them.

The place seemed empty and long deserted. No indication that Don had already arrived. But that, she remembered, was why he had instructed her to bring the key. She hesitated as she reached the door of matched boards. Would it be reckless to go in alone? She wanted to wait for Don. But he would never ask her to do anything that would endanger her. It was bound to be all right.

Resolutely Julie put the key in the lock and turned it. Before she could touch the knob the door swung open quickly, noiselessly, invitingly.

Won't you come into my parlor? said the spider to the fly. Julie's heart crash-dived to the pit of her stomach. Cautiously she peered in. Quiet as a tomb and as eerie. She forced herself to cross the threshold, closed the door and backed up against it, clutching the knob with her right hand.

Sun on the snow outside provided the soft golden glow that illumined the interior. There was a great forge of brick; huge red-leather bellows; a tie rail of nibbled, gnarled oak; iron rims for cart wheels; horseshoes by the rusty score, and a tool-stocked bench. The rich fragrance of cedar was slightly denatured by an acrid smell of smoke.

There was another odor, faint and sweet and familiar. Something white gleamed on the dusty floor. I've dropped my handkerchief, Julie thought, stooped and shoved it into a pocket.

She stood motionless, listening. Her heart pounded out its beat like a hammer on an anvil. What was that? The sound of a woodpile slipping? It came from beyond a door that evidently led to a sort of lean-to.

"Anyone here?" she called softly.

No answer. The sound might have been a squirrel running across the roof. She hoped it was a squirrel. There was something uncanny about the place: queer shadows in the corners, taps on the roof, rodents in the walls. A queer thick smell, as though all the smoke from the old forge were haunting it . . .

The outside light showed up footprints on the dusty floor. Several small ones. Many large ones. One large print was near the slightly open iron door of the firebox of the forge.

Julie's eyes traveled back to the small prints. A woman had been here. She remembered Wheeler saying in an ugly tone to his wife, ''What were you doing at the smithy yesterday afternoon?'' But what could possibly bring that butterfly, that lover of the bright lights, to this dingy spot? There would have to be a powerful motive to drag Clarisse Wheeler here. Everything about the woods frightened her. And yet she had come. Julie was certain of it. And Florence Keane had known.

What could have been the secret bond between the two women? It was concerned in some way, she felt sure, with the odd-shaped medal she had seen in Clarisse's room, the medal that had so interested Captain Holt. But where had he found it and what was its meaning?

In spite of an icy tingle along her veins Julie started for the forge to investigate. Careful as she was, the wide boards of the floor broadcast a creak as she tiptoed across them that sent a tingle along her nerves. She bent to examine the iron door.

''Hands up!''

The low ferocity of that command

slashed the silence. Julie stopped short, slowly raised her arms, turned to face the man who had spoken.

"Lester!"

Though she had seen him only once and then when on the verge of panic, she remembered him clearly. Something had happened to him in the intervening days. He had a heavy growth of beard. He looked famished. His eyes were furtive. He had the quality of a trapped animal. In spite of her fear, Julie felt a twinge of pity for the man.

He wore the woodsman's clothes she had seen on that first encounter. He was bare-headed, a twig caught in his roughened red hair. One hand held a rifle. A hunting rifle? Julie's breath caught in her throat.

He stared at her. "A woman!" he ejaculated as he eyed the slender figure. He set the gun against the wall. "What are you doing here?"

Don, she cried silently. Where are you? Why don't you come? Oh, hurry, hurry!

"Just looking over this New England antiquity." She was pleased to hear how casual her voice sounded.

He laughed jeeringly. Julie saw that he

had lost weight. He was gaunt. What, she wondered, had become of the basket Carrie had packed for him with such loving care? Had he eaten anything since she had been hurt nearly forty-eight hours earlier? He leaned against the wall and she knew it was from sheer weakness.

"Lester," she said impulsively, "why don't you come back with me? You could have a good, hot meal."

His tongue licked out over his lips, he swallowed convulsively, but he did not move.

"Please," she said. "If you are innocent the State Police will help you prove it."

His mouth twisted in a snarl. "They'll convict me of a crime I didn't commit."

"They won't either!" she retorted, thinking of Captain Holt's tired, kindly face.

"Yeah? And even suppose they do let me go. They aren't the only ones after me, or the worst. Not by a long shot. There's not a soul at Blaines' I'd trust as far as I could throw him."

Julie's fear was submerged in anger. "Then you ought to be ashamed of yourself," she raged. "You aren't worth helping. When I think of Carrie defending you the way she did, taking a risk to bring you sandwiches and hot coffee and soup and nearly being killed for it —''

Lester lunged toward her, seized her arm, his eyes boring into hers. ''What's that about Carrie?''

There was no fear in Julie now, only anger and a confused sort of pity. She told him about Carrie's trip in the night with a basket of food, about how someone had struck her down in the snow, leaving her with a concussion of the brain. Lester released her arm, his big hands clenching and unclenching.

''Is she hurt bad?''

''Yes, she's unconscious most of the time. She can't be moved to a hospital. She did all that because she believed in you, Lester, and yet you say there is no one you trust.''

''Carrie is different,'' he mumbled. ''The rest — trying to deprive a working-man of his rights. Ganging up on him. That's the way the system works.''

''It is not!'' Julie's eyes blazed. ''I thought nobody fell for that line but men too lazy or too mentally sick to work. In what country could men reap the reward for their efforts they get here, not just in money and the things that money can buy, but in freedom and independence and being able to live without fear?''

''Without fear!'' He laughed bitterly. ''What do you know about fear? Hiding here — moving on when they look for me — starving —''

''You are running away from something you imagine,'' Julie said crisply. ''The police had no interest in you until you ran away.''

''I wouldn't have had a chance if I had stayed.''

Julie leaned toward him eagerly. ''You do have a chance. Will you take it, Lester? Will you go back to the lodge with me?''

He hesitated. Met her direct eyes.

''For Carrie's sake,'' she added.

''Well — can I trust you, ma'am? Can I?''

''You can,'' Julie assured him.

''All right,'' he agreed. ''I'll go back with you.''

Cr-runch! Cr-runch! Footsteps in the snow. Monty growled and then barked. Lester's eyes were burning dots in skin gone gray.

''And to think I almost believed you,''

he said.

"But —"

The steps were near. "Don't speak," he muttered. "Don't make a sound!" He reached for the rifle propped against the wall.

It seemed to Julie that her throat had closed up. Then she shouted, "Look out! Danger! Don't come in!"

The door swung slowly, slowly open.

ii

Mrs. Blaine and Florence Keane were in the gameroom when Don Bruce appeared. Florence looked up hopefully, then the brightness died out of her face and she turned away.

Mrs. Blaine said solicitously, "You look tired, Don."

He smiled at her. "You always think of other people, don't you? I was tired, but not now. In fact, I'm sitting on top of the world. I've had a talk with the men and they are going back to work in the morning. They've called off the strike."

She clasped her small hands. "That's splendid! How in the world did you accomplish it?''

''Just talked sense to them,'' he told her briefly.

The new maid provided by Captain Holt rolled in the tea wagon.

''You'll join us, won't you, Don?'' Mrs. Blaine said.

''Thank you, but I've got to catch up on some work.''

She spoke to the maid. ''Will you call Miss Ames, please, and tell her that tea is served?''

Don went into the office and looked at the stack of papers and unopened mail that had accumulated in his brief absence. On top was an unstamped envelope addressed to Major Bruce. Who at the Blaine camp, except for Captain Holt, knew his rank? His brows drew together in a frown as he slit open the envelope.

''Don!'' The cry brought him to his feet. Clarisse Wheeler had run into the office. Heavy shadows under her eyes, not artificial, accentuated her pallor.

''What is it, Clarisse?''

She raced around the desk, threw her arms around his neck. She was shaking. ''It's Curtis,'' she sobbed.

''What's wrong with Curtis?''

"He — he struck me! Don, I'm — I'm frightened. Don't let him come near me. I've never seen him like this before. He's mur-murderous."

Don released himself from her clinging embrace and put her in his chair. She was genuinely terrified. At the edge of her jaw a patch of skin was turning dark from a blow.

"You'd better tell me what happened," he said quietly.

"Curtis has been drinking heavily ever since the men went on strike and he couldn't work out of doors. He's always — queer when he is penned up, as he calls it."

Remembering what Wheeler had told him about being in solitary confinement, Don could see why he hated to be indoors. Good Lord, was his wife so dumb she couldn't understand that, or so self-centered that she just did not care?

"He's been getting worse and worse," she sobbed. "Just now he came up to our room and accused me of k-killing Swen Oorth. He said I was the one who made the scratches on Swen's face. He said I'd been meeting him, that I'd had an affair with him, that he'd seen me outside the smithy the afternoon of the day Oorth was shot, and later saw Oorth come out.''

Clarisse looked up, her face ugly and swollen from tears, but with malice in her small eyes. ''Well, it's true. Partly, anyhow. I *was* having an affair with Swen,'' she said defiantly. ''A woman likes a man to pay attention to her and all Curtis cared about was his job. But the funny thing is that the one time Curtis thought he had caught me, I wasn't with Swen. I had gone down to the smithy because I suspected Swen was two-timing me. The woman in the smithy with him was Florence Keane. They were quarreling. She was the one who made those scratches on his face. I heard him yell when she did it and curse at her.''

A breath was sharply drawn. Don looked up to see Charlie Keane pause at the doorway and then go on. Don turned back to Clarisse, wondering if she knew the harm she had done, wondering whether she would care if she knew.

''Go fix your face and have tea in the gameroom,'' he said shortly. ''Wheeler won't bother you while you are with Mrs. Blaine. I'll have a talk with him later.''

When Clarisse had gone, Don ran his

hand through his hair and turned back to the envelope on his desk addressed to Major Bruce.

It was brief and to the point: *Leave here at once or something will happen to Julie Ames*. There was no signature.

"Don," Mrs. Blaine had come into the office. "You have so much on your mind I hate to trouble you but — my dear!" she broke off. "What is wrong? You are dead white."

Don struggled for control. "What is the matter, Mrs. Blaine?"

"Julie isn't in the house. No one saw her leave and it is getting so dark I can't help worrying."

He pushed past her to the hall closet, jerked on a Mackinaw and cap, boots and gloves. He was opening the front door when she called, "Monty must be with her."

It was very dark. He came back for a light and fastened it to his belt. Went down the steps. Whistled. Waited and listened. Whistled again.

In the distance he heard Monty's frenzied barking. He began to run. Led by the sound of the dog's bark, he went down the road, past the pond, and then picked up the small footprints in the snow. Where on earth could Julie have been going alone? Or had she been lured away by the person who had left the anonymous warning on his desk?

Julie in the hands of a murderer! And now he knew, beyond doubt, who the murderer was. Julie with the near-black hair, the deep pansy-soft eyes, the skin like a flower. Julie with her courage and her laughter.

The footprints led toward the deserted smithy. Surely she could not have gone there. Or had she been taken by force? No, there was only one set of footprints.

Something was jumping up and down frantically. Something brown. Monty launched himself at Don, yipping distractedly.

"Quiet," Don said. "Quiet, old boy."

The snow crunched under his heavy boots.

And from inside the smithy Julie shouted, "Look out! Danger! Don't come in!"

XVI

THE DOOR swung slowly, slowly open. Julie's eyes widened as she watched it. Lester was raising the rifle. Monty poked in his brown nose, followed in a moment by Don Bruce. Without pausing for thought, Julie flung her weight on Lester's arm so suddenly that the rifle clattered to the ground.

The dog and the man seemed to leap at the same moment. There was a brief sharp tussle and then Don shouted, "Down, Monty! Call him off, Julie. Everything's under control."

Julie called to the dog and finally tugged at his collar. Reluctantly Monty abandoned his grip on Lester's leg, growling low in his throat.

Don, holding Lester by an arm twisted behind his back, reached for a leather strap hanging on the wall and tied his prisoner's hands behind him. Then he stood back, panting. When he spoke, Julie was taken aback.

"Really, Lester," he said in a casual, friendly tone, "what an idiot you are to make so much trouble for yourself and for us. Who scared you into running away?"

"No one," Lester said promptly.

"You're a fool not to tell me, you know. Up to now, you haven't done much irreparable harm, but to protect a killer is a different business, a very serious one."

"I'm not!" Lester was startled.

"Then why did you run away?"

"So I wouldn't be killed."

"Who told you that you'd be killed?"

"I'm not talking," Lester said sullenly.

"We'll see what Captain Holt has to say to that," Don warned him.

"That's right," Lester snarled. "Bring on your third degree."

Don laughed. "Someone has really been talking down the American system to you — and, boy, how you fell for it! Come on."

He turned to Julie and her heart leaped at the expression in his eyes. "Are you all right?''

''Yes, he didn't hurt me.''

''But, why did you leave the house alone?''

''Because — didn't you write this note?'' As she saw his blank astonishment Julie dug the note from her pocket. As she pulled it out, something white fluttered to the ground. Don stooped, picked it up, looked at it and then absently dropped it into his own pocket instead of returning it to her.

He read the note, his face as hard as a rock. ''So that's how it was done!'' He took a long uneven breath. ''I don't need to tell you I didn't write that note, though it's a fairly good imitation of my handwriting.'' He summoned up a smile to drive the horror from her face. ''After this we'll have to arrange some private signals for identification. When I write to you I'll never be satisfied to say 'Love.' I'll say, 'I adore you.' ''

Blood rushed into her pale face and then she met the laughter in his eyes. She managed a wavering smile. ''I'll tie a knot in my handkerchief so I can remember to look for it,'' she said demurely and laughter shone in her own eyes.

"You are a brave little soldier," he told her huskily. "You go ahead with Monty where I can keep an eye on you. Lester and I will bring up the rear."

"Where are you taking me?" Lester demanded.

Don chuckled. "Why, to get that third degree, of course. Captain Holt generally uses thumbscrews and a torture rack but he's fresh out of them right now."

Lester had the grace to blush.

Outside, Julie drew the sharp resinous air deep into her lungs. It helped dispel the sense of nightmare. A crimson light spread in the west as they tramped homeward along the shining black road.

The walk back to the lodge was a silent one. Who, Julie was wondering, wrote me that note? Why was I sent to the smithy?

What, Don was wondering, would have happened to Julie if I had not found her in time? Someone intended that she should not return. She was to be held prisoner until I promised to withdraw from the case. Or perhaps she was to have been sacrificed ruthlessly. But what had delayed the writer of the note? Oh, of course. By chance, the smithy had been chosen for the rendezvous and Lester was hiding in the smithy, an unforeseen complication. Don reached in his pocket and pulled out the handkerchief Julie had dropped. Where on earth had she got hold of it? The initials were F.K., Florence Keane.

What, Lester was wondering in despair, would happen now? Would he be arrested for the murder of Swen Oorth? Had the girl deliberately tracked him down at the smithy or had she told him the truth? Had Carrie really been injured while she had been trying to help him? Why would she take such a risk for his sake? Did it mean that she cared for a roughneck like him, that she believed in him? What chance would he have if he told the truth? That was the big question. None, he thought. None at all. He would be destroyed, as Downing and Oorth had been destroyed, when they became a menace. What a fool he had been! What an awful fool. And now, if he weren't arrested on a murder charge he would be set free by the police, turned loose so that the Other One could get at him. And that would be the end of Lester.

Only once was the silence broken on the

walk home. Don said, "Monty rates a decoration for this day's work. I lived a year, Julie, from the time I followed your footprints in the snow, till I heard your voice and the door swung open, and I saw you backed up against the forge."

There was a State Police car outside the house and Captain Holt was sitting in the office as they trooped in, talking to Mrs. Blaine.

"This is Captain Holt of the State Police," Don said quietly to his captive. "I brought our missing friend Lester along, Captain, to answer some questions."

"Not yet," Mrs. Blaine broke in. "The poor man is half frozen and half starved. He must get warm and have something to eat first."

Lester glanced at the police officer, expecting that the latter would protest. Instead, Holt said, "That's a good idea, Mrs. Blaine. Come up to the fire, man, where you can thaw out. Take off that strap, Bruce. He won't try to run away again."

Lester huddled close to the fire, his teeth chattering. In a few minutes Mrs. Blaine came back with a cup of tea and a plate of sandwiches. ''This isn't a real meal,'' she explained, ''but at least the tea is hot and the sandwiches will hold you until supper is ready.''

She turned to Julie. ''Run up and see Carrie, will you, dear? She is better but she has been asking for you. But don't stay too long. Talking tires her and makes her head ache.''

''Maybe,'' Lester said slowly, ''maybe I got the wrong slant on you.''

''Just a minute,'' Captain Holt intervened as Julie was about to leave the room. ''No one was around when you came in. Shut the office door when you leave, Miss Ames, so no one will see Lester or guess that he is here. Is that clear?''

Julie nodded, though it wasn't in the least clear. After all the fuss about looking for Lester, why keep the fact that he had been found a secret?

ii

Carrie was conscious when the nurse admitted Julie to her room, her eyes wide open but too bright and staring, as a result of shock. Her head moved restlessly on the pillows.

"I want to speak to Miss Ames alone," she said.

Ann Adams, the nurse provided by Captain Holt, spoke cheerfully but firmly. "You can talk to Miss Ames for exactly ten minutes, but the cap — the doctor gave me strict instructions not to leave you alone at any time or under any pretext."

At Carrie's gesture Julie knelt beside the bed, close to the sick woman, who whispered, "What has happened to Lester?"

"We found him."

Carrie started in alarm and Julie's hand covered hers. "Don't worry. I think everything will be all right if —"

"If?" Carrie lifted herself on her pillows and then clutched at her throbbing head.

"If Lester will only tell the truth. Captain Holt does not really believe he is guilty but if he persists in refusing to talk, there won't be much choice for the police. They'll have to arrest him."

"I'll make him talk," Carrie said suddenly.

Julie smiled. "I hope you can do it. And now don't worry about him. He is going to have a nourishing hot supper and the best of care. He's far better off now than if he were hiding in the woods and moving from shelter to shelter. He'll be safe, too, and more at peace in his mind."

Carrie looked at her in gratitude and relief. "I'd like to tell you about it," she said softly. "It's been preying on my mind but I just didn't know if I could trust anyone. I know I can trust you, though." Her eyes closed for a moment and then she opened them and began to talk quickly, in a low tone, so that the nurse would not overhear her.

"The night Oorth was killed I was in the kitchen. I heard the shot before Monty began to bark. I could see clearly out to the cabin. Lester was there — and someone else. The other one was out of range of the light but I could see the gleam of the rifle barrel when it was moved. I knew something awful had happened.

"I could tell somehow when Lester was alone and the other one had gone. Lester turned toward the house and his face was so — so despairing. I opened the door and called him. He said Oorth had been killed

302

but he didn't dare tell who had shot him or he'd be next. He had to get away. He was about frantic; he didn't make sense. I gave him some coffee and made some sandwiches real quick and then pretended to have a headache and slipped out to show him where he could hide. I knew he wouldn't last long out in that blizzard. There's an old dugout that used to be an ice cellar for keeping milk and butter, before this place was electrified. I guess people had just forgotten that it existed. I got Lester some blankets and sent him down there. Only — there are rats. I couldn't bear it for him.

''The next day when the police came he began to move around from place to place. He realized if he was found in the dugout people would know I'd told him. I was the only one who remembered about it. Then I got a note about meeting him with food. That's when I pretended to have the toothache. I went out with a basket and someone followed me.''

There was horror in Carrie's face and her hands clung to Julie's. The girl remembered the shadow she had seen while she was making her way to the smithy and clasped Carrie's feverish hands tight in her own.

"Just as I came toward the place where I was to meet Lester," the sick woman went on, "I could see Lester standing beside a tree. I had to warn him. I yelled and he ran away. I wanted to give him time to escape and I turned around. I couldn't see the other one, because he kept edging behind me, but I tried to trip him up and then — that's all I remember until I opened my eyes and I was here in bed."

"Time," the nurse said briskly.

Julie bent over and spoke quickly. "I told Lester that you believed in him and what you did for him."

A smile curved Carrie's lips, made her almost radiant. "Someday," she promised, "I'll pay my debt to you. Some way."

Julie went into her own room and locked the door. She sank down wearily in a chair and then jumped to her feet. Carrie was better and Lester had been found: surely everything was under control. She chose a dress of turquoise taffeta. It was time to chase the gloom away from the lodge and replace it by a little gaiety.

She waited until the Keanes and the Wheelers had gone downstairs and then ran down herself. They were all assembled in the gameroom except for Captain Holt and Lester. Aunt Deb's eyes were too bright but Don stood beside her chair, watching her vigilantly, a finger resting on her pulse.

Curtis Wheeler whistled as he caught sight of Julie. "How about that dance date we had?" he demanded.

"I am looking forward to it," Julie declared.

"That's a fine idea," Don said enthusiastically. "Our troubles are over. Lester has been arrested. Captain Holt has locked him up in Oorth's old cabin for the night and gone back to headquarters. He has been missing a lot of sleep and decided to postpone questioning Lester until tomorrow. He has called off all his men. Tonight we'll celebrate."

Julie started to speak and met the warning in Don's eyes. Why was he lying? she wondered. The nurse, the cook, the houseman — all these had been provided by the captain, and they were still at the lodge. Judging by the nurse's refusal to leave Carrie alone, they were definitely on guard duty.

However, Don's announcement served the purpose. There was a general lift in spirits. For the first time since her arrival, supper was a gay affair. The release of tension made everyone talk and laugh. Banter was tossed lightly from table to table like a ping-pong ball. Julie, watching it all, thought anyone would believe these were carefree people without a worry in the world. And yet — and yet one of them was a murderer who had killed two men, nearly killed Carrie, and twice — three times — had attempted to kill her. Which one? Which one?

When they had returned to the game-room Curtis Wheeler stacked dance records on the turntable, pushed back the rugs and held out his arms to Julie. ''Now, Glamour Girl,'' he began.

Outside a car started up.

''Who's that?'' Charlie Keane asked quickly.

''The couple who are doing the house-work are off for the movie in the village,'' Don explained easily.

Julie's eyes flickered toward him. Something was happening or about to happen. Don's face was inscrutable.

"Well," Charlie Keane said, "Lester has made clear he was the guy Holt wants."

"Are you sure of that?" Don asked.

"What do you mean?"

"I'd like to talk to you, Keane. You, too, Florence."

"What has my wife got to —" Charlie began angrily.

Don made no comment. He waited. Slowly, Florence went out of the room and her husband followed. Don brought up the rear. In a moment the door of the office closed behind them.

XVII

WHEN he had closed the door of the office Don turned to the silent couple.

"We won't be too official about this," he said easily. He pulled an easy chair close to the fire for Florence, waved Keane toward another, and leaned against the mantel looking at them.

Unexpectedly, he put his hand in his pocket and pulled out the odd-shaped medal. He held it for Charlie Keane's inspection.

"Ever see that before?" he asked.

Keane picked it up, turned it over curiously, returned it. "No," he said. "What is it?"

Don held it out to Florence. "What about you?"

It did not seem possible that she could turn any paler. "Yes," she said, "I've seen it before."

"Tell me what you know about it, Florence. Everything you know about it."

"Just a minute," Keane intervened. "I'd like to know by what right you are questioning my wife Florence, you needn't answer because Bruce has no authority here. I'll get you a lawyer."

"But I want to answer, Charlie," she replied. "These last few days I've learned there is nothing so terrible as silence, as things that are left unsaid." She turned to Don. "I can't really tell you much about this medal. All I know is that it belonged to Swen Oorth."

Don gave a muffled exclamation of incredulity. "Are you sure of that, Florence?"

Something in his tone puzzled her. "Well," she said slowly, "he was skiing with me one day and I took a spill. He bent over to pull me up and this medal fell out of his pocket. He made an awful fuss about digging the thing out of the snow. Said it was his lucky piece."

"His lucky piece! Good Lord," Don exclaimed, "how tragically wrong can a man be! Did you ever see it after that?"

"Only once. It was on Clarisse

Wheeler's dressing-table the day Swen was killed. I assumed he had given it to her. I think that is the impression she wanted me to have, at any rate.''

Don slipped the medal back in his pocket. Again he took the Keanes by surprise. ''Charlie, what happened to you in Korea?''

''That,'' Keane said evenly, ''does not concern you, Bruce.''

''As a matter of fact,'' Don told him, ''it concerns me far more than your performance of your job here as superintendent.''

''I don't understand you.''

''Then it is time you did.'' Don's eyes moved from Keane's face with its sudden look of strain to Florence who sat unmoving, frozen, remote. ''It's time you did.'' In as few words as possible, he explained his presence at the Blaine lodge.

''You mean,'' Charlie said at last, ''that you don't think Lester killed Oorth. You believe it was one of us.'' Something in his tone brought Florence's head up alertly. She was about to speak when Don stopped her with a peremptory, warning gesture.

''I mean,'' he said distinctly, ''that I

310

am not simply trying to run down a murderer. I am looking for a traitor. Unless you want to be tarred with that brush —''

''My God,'' Charlie Keane cried out, horrified, ''you can't think —''

''Of course he doesn't,'' Florence exclaimed indignantly, ''no one would ever believe it for a single minute.''

''Quiet, Florence,'' Don said sharply. ''You see the situation, Keane. Unless you care to tell me what happened to you in Korea, you will inevitably be under suspicion as a Communist and a traitor to your country.''

Charlie Keane was silent for a long time. ''I can't let such a suspicion rest on my name,'' he groaned at last. ''Anything is better than dishonor. I had hoped I would never have to drag all this out into the daylight but there seems to be no choice. All I ask is that Florence leave and I tell you this alone.''

''I want Florence to stay,'' Don decided quietly.

Charlie Keane yielded with an exhausted sigh. He leaned close to the fire, his eyes and most of his face shielded by his hand. ''All right,'' he conceded in a dead voice from which all hope was gone, "I suppose this is best. Sooner or later, it had to come out. And, in a way, it's not important any longer —" He broke off and for a long time he was sunk deep in his thoughts. Neither Don nor Florence stirred.

"I suppose," Keane began, "you've wondered why Florence ever married me. I always wondered, too. She is beautiful and she is immensely rich. She had everything. I had nothing. We met in Switzerland where I was a news photographer. We were guests at the same skiing party. Florence is crazy about all kinds of sports and at that time — Well, I was good at them, too. I fell in love with her and we got married. We were together only a few months before I was called into the Armed Services."

He was silent again for a long time. "It was all right while I was in training and even when I was fighting. There were her letters to live on. But later I was captured — and there were no more letters. I had time to think for the first time about how rich she was and that I had nothing to offer her. Nothing we could share but an interest in sports. And finally," he was looking at the fire now, avoiding his wife's eyes, "I got into trouble. I helped several of the guys escape, and the Reds knew it. They wanted to find out how the escapes were being managed. But there were half a dozen men still waiting to try it and to tell the Reds would be to push these men right into the hands of the enemy. So I couldn't talk and they — tortured me."

Florence covered her mouth with her hand, a little moan in her throat.

"It went on," Charlie said expressionlessly, "for quite a while. When they got through with me I knew, though I could walk all right, there were no more sports for me. And Florence liked them so much. I didn't want her to find out because then she would realize we had nothing in common. Well, we were released and Mrs. Blaine offered me this job and I had only my army pay so I took it. Florence came along like a good sport."

"A good sport!" she said in a choked voice. She had left her chair, she was kneeling beside him. No one, Don thought, smiling, would call her frozen now. Her face was warm, vivid, lovely. "Charlie! Look at me, darling! I married you because I loved you. The money didn't matter. Ever. The sports didn't matter. All that shamed me was that I wasn't clever enough for you, and when you came back — changed — I thought," there was a sobbing laugh, "you were sorry you had married me because I was so stupid. And when Swen Oorth asked me to ski I went because you didn't care for me any more. But that's all there was to it. He never even kissed me. Just that last day, he asked me to meet him at the smithy —"

"Don't talk, Florence," he warned her in anguish.

"Let her talk," Don said. "Don't you understand that it's all right, old man?"

Florence went on. "He pretended he had something to tell me about you. And then he tried to make love to me. And I — I scratched his face! Clarisse had followed us; she saw the whole thing. But I didn't kill him. I never saw him again."

"But why did you faint when you heard that he was dead?"

"Because — because —"

"You were afraid I had done it! Oh, Florence —"

Their arms were around each other, she

was sobbing on his shoulder. They had forgotten Don. He went quietly to the door. As he opened it he heard Charlie Keane whisper, ''Don't cry, my beloved. Don't cry. All's well with us.''

ii

Curtis Wheeler ran his hand under his collar. ''Let's get out on the porch if you've got to talk. I'm stifling in here. Feels as though the walls were closing in on me.''

''All right,'' Don agreed.

The two men put on heavy coats, pulled wool caps down over their ears and went out into the icy cold. The night was so black that they could not see even the porch railing, but the sky was brilliant with stars, lemon-colored stars that quivered and danced as though shivering with the cold.

Wheeler did not seem to mind. He filled his lungs with the icy air and his tension relaxed. After the two men had paced the length of the porch several times in silence he said, ''Okay, you can go ahead, Bruce. That solitary confinement in prison camp seems to have left me with a kind of claustrophobia. When I am indoors too long I don't seem able to breathe. What's on your mind?''

Bruce paused, switched on the flashlight that was hooked to his belt, held the medal in its beam.

''What do you know about that, Wheeler?''

The big man looked at it in silence. He did not pick it up or attempt to examine it closely. ''Never saw it before,'' he said curtly.

''Perhaps we'll save time if I tell you that it was seen by two witnesses on your wife's dressing table the afternoon of the day Oorth died,'' Don told him.

''All right,'' Wheeler groaned. ''That's where I found the thing. Made Clarisse explain what it was. She said Oorth had given it to her. He asked her to take it for safekeeping. Then, when we knew he was dead, I didn't want her tied up with him in any way. I — I threw it down beside his body that night in the cabin. I wanted to shield her if I could.''

''I think that was probably the truth, you know,'' Don said, feeling profoundly sorry for the man whose wife had been unfaithful, wanting to save him from hearing the ugly truth if he could. "I mean, Oorth probably did ask her to put it away for him. It was a very dangerous thing to have in his possession. So dangerous that even parting with it could not save him."

"I don't know what you are talking about," Wheeler said bluntly.

"Let's try being honest with each other," Don suggested. "You are afraid Clarisse killed Oorth. She's afraid you did. That's why she had hysterics."

"Then you don't believe she is the one who murdered him?"

Don shook his head and then realized that Wheeler could not see his gesture in the dark. "No, Clarisse didn't do it."

"Thank heaven!" the superintendent said fervently. "Don't misunderstand me, Bruce. Clarisse and I are washed up. All that kept me sane in prison camp was thinking that my wife would be waiting when I got out. Well," he took a long breath, "you can guess what I found. Coming up here was a sort of last chance. And then she played around with Oorth. I knew then that nothing could be salvaged from our marriage. There was only one thing left and that was to go our separate ways. Clarisse could return to the bright lights and I'd stay here, working out of doors in the woods I love. Then Oorth died, and I thought Clarisse had killed him from jealousy. I had to protect her the best I knew how. After all, she was my wife, I had loved her once, and I was still responsible for her. But if she is clear —''

''She is clear and so are you, Wheeler. By the way, how would you like to take over my job as manager when I leave here?''

''Manager! Do you mean that?''

''Don!'' Julie had flung open the door. ''Captain Holt telephoned. He wants you to come to headquarters as soon as possible.''

''Now what?'' muttered Wheeler.

''Lester,'' Don said sadly, ''and the last act of the play.''

XVIII

NOW AND THEN Julie turned a page in her book but she had no idea what the lines of print meant. Since she had received the telephone call for Don from Captain Holt, the evening that was to have been so gay had been a dismal failure. Indeed, it had been a failure from the time when Don had taken Charlie and Florence Keane into the office. After a long time the Keanes had gone upstairs. They had never returned to the gameroom.

Then Don and Curtis Wheeler had gone out on the porch. Clarisse, never happy unless she was the center of masculine attention, had moved restlessly around the gameroom, and finally had forced the reluctant Hugh to dance with her, his wistful eyes following Julie while he dipped and turned and sidestepped with Clarisse in his arms. He was released at length by a casual comment of Mrs. Blaine's.

"The new cook is awfully upset because there are rats in the cellar where we keep our supplies."

"I'll set some traps," Hugh offered eagerly.

That was when the telephone had rung; Julie had answered it and given Don the message from Captain Holt. Curtis Wheeler had returned to the gameroom and offered to help Hugh with the traps in the cellar. He, too, seemed anxious to escape from Clarisse, who had stormed off upstairs.

"I'll be in touch with you as soon as I know what it is all about," Don had promised Julie before he left. "Something new must have come up. Everything," he added cryptically, "was all set."

Since then, Julie and her aunt had kept their silent vigil by the fire. Julie looked up to find her aunt watching her with a troubled face. She closed her book at once.

"What is worrying you, Aunt Deb?"

"You are. Ever since Quentin sent me that telegram, saying that you had broken

320

your engagement to him and were going to marry Don instead, I've been worried. Not that I have anything against Don," she added hastily, "but you've known each other such a short time. Are you sure you understand him well enough, love him enough —"

"It wasn't really an engagement." Julie described the scene on the dance floor of the roof restaurant. "That's all there was to it," she concluded. "Quentin was being impossible and making a scene, so Don shut him off."

Her aunt studied her for a moment and then her lips curved in a smile. "Come here, child."

With a soft rustle of the long taffeta skirt Julie came to kneel beside her aunt's chair. A thin blue-veined hand tilted the girl's chin upward so that Aunt Deb could look into her eyes.

"Are you sure," she asked softly, "that's all there is to it?"

Color flamed in Julie's cheeks, her lips quivered, but her eyes were steady. "No," she said honestly, "that's not all. I love him, Aunt Deb. With all my heart. For always."

Her aunt did not speak. She touched the

girl's glowing cheek gently with her hand. Julie continued to kneel beside her, content to look at the fire and dream. Most of the time she felt sure that Don loved her as she loved him. But, after all, he had not said so. And yet, if he did not return her love, nothing in life made any sense. And suppose he did —

At length the older woman got to her feet. "Don't stay up too late, dear," she said, and went out to climb the stairs slowly to her room.

Julie still knelt beside the chair, deep in her dreams. An airplane motor throbbed overhead and was gone, making her aware how still the night was, how still the lodge was. There was no sound from her aunt's room, no sound anywhere. Hugh and Curtis were still presumably setting traps in the cellar. They had been gone a long time.

That made her realize that Don, too, had been gone a long time. With the roads open, it should not take more than half an hour to reach State Police headquarters.

The woodbox was empty and the room was growing chilly. She got up and began to pace the length of the room, her skirt rustling as she walked. There was something going on that she had not been told. After keeping Lester's capture a secret, Don had announced publicly that he had been arrested and that he was locked in Oorth's cabin. He had pretended that Captain Holt had withdrawn his people. Or was it pretense? Had the houseman and the cook really left for the movies? What was she to believe?

She walked from the window, which reflected only the blackness of the night, to the dying fire on the hearth, which reflected the castles in Spain she had been erecting. A long time passed. Don had been gone nearly three hours.

An impulse she could not control drove her into the office to the telephone. He'll be furious with me for making a fuss, she told herself. Men don't like women who fuss. But I can't help it.

She dialed State Police headquarters and asked for Captain Holt. It was a blessed relief to hear the familiar voice say, "What can I do for you, Miss Ames?"

"I hope I'm not a nuisance," she apologized. "Could be I'm a little hysterical or something. I was beginning to worry because Don — Mr. Bruce hasn't come back.''

''Come back!'' There was a moment of strained silence and then Holt said sharply, ''Where did he go, Miss Ames?''

''He left for headquarters as soon as I gave him your message.'' She was startled.

''I didn't send any message,'' Holt told her. ''And Bruce never reached here.'' She heard his voice in the background giving staccato orders, then it came on again. ''Hold everything, Miss Ames. I'm on my way.''

Julie put down the telephone. She looked blankly around her. Something had happened to Don as it had happened to Downing and Swen Oorth. Somewhere in the night Don Bruce was lying injured or — or . . .

You've got to think, she told herself firmly, holding down panic. You can't afford to lose your head. But she had no plan, only an unswerving resolve to find him. Something that was deeper than reason, something as deep as instinct, guided her. There was no time to lose. Every nerve in her body told her that. Don had to be found and found at once.

She ran down the cellar stairs. The lights were on but there was no sign of Wheeler or Gordon. She called them, her voice echoing back at her mockingly. No answer.

She ran up to her room, kicked off high-heeled slippers, took off her dress, got into ski suit and heavy shoes, pulled on cap and gloves and galoshes, caught up a flashlight.

She must tell someone where she was going. Not Aunt Deb. The men had disappeared. She tapped softly on Carrie's door. The nurse was one of Captain Holt's people. She would know what to do.

There was no answer. She tapped again. Turned the knob. Went inside. The covers were thrown back on the bed. Carrie was gone. So was the nurse, Miss Adams.

This was nightmare. Everyone seemed to have vanished, leaving Julie alone with horror.

Something white was pinned to the back of a chair, a note addressed to her:

Miss Ames, my patient tricked me. Sent me down to the kitchen for hot milk. When I came back, she had disappeared. I've gone to look for her. Please notify Captain Holt.

ANN ADAMS

Julie raced down the stairs, out the front door. She had not realized the night would be so cold, so dark. She turned on the flashlight and made her way to the garage. Don would certainly have taken the convertible.

The garage doors were open and she stood blinking in surprise. The estate wagon was gone and the convertible was there. She tried to think. Then it was true that the servants had gone to the movies, taken the estate wagon. But how had Don gone to the State Police headquarters? There was no other car.

Her heart was pounding wildly. *Don had never left the place.* She went back along the driveway, switching the light from side to side, casting it under bushes. But he could not be here, she remembered, or Monty would have raised an alarm. Her search had taken her back almost to the lodge. Should she go in and telephone the State Police again? No use. Captain Holt was on his way. But he would be too late. Why, why, had he called off his people at the time when they were most needed?

She turned, went back, searching more carefully. She was sobbing now. Don! Don! Where are you! What happened to you? Where are the men? Where is every-one? Don!

A deeper shadow in the shadow of a tree trunk . . . She bent over, knees shaking so they could barely support her. Her hand touched something furry. Monty! She crouched beside the motionless body, brought the light close. Tears streamed down her cheeks. Monty would never again sound the alarm. His head had been crushed. The faithful little fellow was dead.

Julie scrambled to her feet, faint and sick. Monty had been killed so that he would not let them know that Don — Don . . .

She went into the garage once more, her light moving slowly, foot by foot. Was that — No, that was a workbench. That — No, it was a pile of sponges and cleaning rags. That — that body swaying in the air? One hand fastened over her heart to still the mad pounding that seemed to shake her whole body. No, that was a pair of overalls used in working on the cars. She sagged against the wall in her relief.

Yet something in her mind cried, *Hurry! Hurry!* She had examined every foot of the garage. Everything but the convertible itself. She opened the door. No one. Nothing. . . . There was a creaking sound and she switched off her light. Listened. Nothing but the wind. She turned on the light again. She had looked everywhere. No, there was one place left, the luggage compartment. She went behind the car. Glory be! The lid wasn't locked. She lifted it. Saw the man lying with his legs drawn up, eyes closed, face parchment-white.

"Don!" She touched his face. "Don!" She bent over until her cheek rested against his cold one. His breath faintly stirred a lock of her hair. Unconscious but still breathing. "Don!" She put her arms around him, holding him. "Don, dearest."

There was a movement behind her and Julie screamed, wildly, loudly, again and again, the sounds ripping through the night silence like a knife cutting through a silk fabric.

All of a sudden the garage lights blazed

on and the place was crowded with people. There was the new houseman, a businesslike revolver in his hand; there was Curtis Wheeler, out of breath from running; there was Hugh Gordon, crying, "What is it, Julie? What happened? What made you scream?" There was Charlie Keane.

The houseman and Wheeler lifted Don and carried him into the house. The former put him on the couch in the gameroom and examined him quickly. "Nothing broken, so far as I can tell," he said. "He just got a nasty knock on the head." He lifted Don's head gently and let brandy trickle down his throat.

Don choked, swallowed, opened his eyes. Almost before he was completely conscious they were searching for Julie, found her. "Told you — stay inside — take care of yourself," he mumbled with difficulty.

"What happened to you, Don?"

"Someone waiting at the garage. All that saved me was the fact that I'd tucked my notes on the case inside my cap. Thought someone might try to stop me, might search me. Those notes softened the blow."

"Do you know who did it?" the house-man asked.

"Oh, yes," Don said. "I know. But I can't prove it — without Lester."

XIX

THEY had all gathered in the gameroom: Florence and Charlie Keane, looking as though they were living in a separate world from the others, as though nothing that happened here could concern them; Curtis and Clarisse Wheeler, the former alert, ready to spring into action, the latter frightened and bewildered; Hugh Gordon and Don Bruce, standing side by side in front of the fireplace, for Don had resolutely refused to remain on the couch to which he had been carried; Mrs. Blaine sitting erect in her high-backed chair, smiling valiantly at Julie with chalk-white lips; Lester, with a police guard on either side of him; Carrie with her nurse; the houseman and cook with Captain Holt and four more troopers, all looking grim and alert, their hands close to their holsters;

and — and — Julie stared unbelievingly — Quentin Harrington, who stood blinking around him in amazement. Quentin's overcoat had been tossed over a chair arm; there were two suitcases at his feet. Evidently he had come to stay until he could persuade Julie to leave with him.

Captain Holt exchanged a look with Don, nodded and stepped back. ''It's all yours, Bruce,'' he said. ''Take it away.''

The troopers moved unobtrusively until they were guarding the door and the windows, standing so that they had an unobstructed view of everyone in the room. And suddenly the atmosphere changed. The time had come to end the long nightmare. But the awakening, Julie thought, would be worse than the dream itself. These men were highly trained, deadly serious. When they stretched out their hands someone — someone in this room who was still free — would leave it manacled, a prisoner, to go on trial for his life. Or her life.

The girl's heart pounded heavily, so heavily it seemed to her the others in the room must hear it as they could hear the steady ticking of the tall clock in the hallway. Her breath was rapid and shallow.

She kept her eyes down because she dared not look around at the other faces, afraid of what she might see in one of them.

Only Quentin was insensitive to the atmosphere, to the anguished expectancy of the group. He looked around, puzzled by finding so many people, outraged by the presence of the troopers.

"What's going on here?" he demanded. "Julie, I've come to take you home. I chartered a plane and came from the airfield by taxi. Fortunately, it's still waiting. Come along at once."

"Not now," Julie told him. "Can't you see — something is happening."

"Keep still, whoever you are," Captain Holt said in a tone of such authority that Quentin subsided.

Don stood with one hand in his pocket, the other resting lightly on Hugh's shoulder. The latter looked younger than usual, perhaps because, for the first time, Don looked old. Old and sad.

"This story," Don began quietly, "goes back a long time, months as I know it, perhaps years so far as the criminal is concerned. Back to an unhappy childhood and an accumulation of resentments that ended in a feeling of abuse, of being misunderstood and mistreated. All of these things our criminal blamed on circumstances, on luck, on the system under which he lived, on everything but himself. So when the Reds tried their propaganda on him they found a willing tool, ready to believe he had been wronged, eager to take his revenge.''

There was a faint stir as Florence Keane turned to smile at her husband, and his hand closed over hers. They seemed to be standing within a charmed circle, untouched by what was happening in the room.

''I came into the story in Korea when I was a prisoner,'' Don's voice went on. ''On the day I was released . . .'' He described the conversation he had accidentally overheard; how he had learned that one of the men being returned to his own country was coming back as a Communist, an organizer, a troublemaker.

Clarisse gasped. ''Is that why . . . Curtis, did you . . . ?''

''Keep still,'' he growled. ''You double-crossing little . . .''

Captain Holt looked at the Wheelers and they fell silent.

''The worst of it,'' Don went on, ''was

that I had absolutely no way of telling which man it was. I lost the trail completely for some weeks, picked it up by sheer accident, and followed it here to the Blaine lodge.

"By the time of my arrival, I realized that our criminal had already been very active. He had made the loggers feel that they were badly treated and he had acquired an ardent recruit. But somewhere he had slipped up. Someone guessed what he was doing. That someone, I hardly need tell you, was Downing. So Downing was killed.

"Nearly all criminals find that one false step leads to another and another, until there is no turning back. Downing had been silenced and no suspicion attached to our killer. But no one in the village believed in that hunting accident. Instead, there was a growing conviction that the manager had been murdered and the truth was being covered up. So our criminal looked around for a second line of defense, for someone to take the blame for Downing's murder if it should become necessary. He found what he needed in Lester."

Standing between his guards, Lester

slumped, head sinking forward on his chest, looking down to avoid the curious eyes that turned to him.

''He didn't know what he was doing,'' Carrie cried out, her voice shaking from weakness. ''He didn't know. Honest, he didn't.''

The passionate conviction in her faint voice brought Lester's head up momentarily. His eyes met hers. He summoned up a rueful smile.

Don went on talking. ''How he worked on Lester, only Lester can tell us, but he hid behind him. It was Lester who handed out the propaganda to the men, Lester who did the dirty work.''

Lester's big fist clenched and one of the troopers guarding him stiffened alertly. With a bitter expression Lester let his hand drop limply to his side.

''Again the criminal felt secure, and again he found there was no security for a man like him. He carried an odd-shaped medal with the numbers 876 scratched on it. That medal, as Newton Brewster has ascertained from the Washington Bureau of the F.B.I., is a new method of identification used by Red organizers in this country. In some way Swen Oorth found that medal and knew what the man was. It seems likely that Oorth, too, had been approached by the enemy, because he was obviously not a very solid citizen. But he had not fallen that low, though he was low enough to use the knowledge he had acquired in an attempt at blackmail.''

I don't know Don at all, Julie thought, watching his stern face, hearing that cold, impersonal voice. No wonder Mr. Brewster said he was dangerous. Nothing will swerve him now until justice has been done. Nothing. She looked away from his face to Hugh's. Like the others he was listening intently. Don's mention of Oorth's blackmail had made him angry. He shifted his weight, caught Julie's eyes and smiled.

''The criminal knew that Oorth, like Downing, had to be silenced. But how was it to be done? Another unexplained death might bring his house of cards down upon his head. But he had a perfect fall guy at hand: Lester, who was pulling his chestnuts out of the fire. He stirred up a quarrel between Lester and Oorth and, knowing Oorth had gone to meet Miss Ames at the station, arranged to have Lester fell a tree across the road and kill him as he returned. Lester did not know about Miss Ames's presence in the sleigh.

"Well, the attempt failed, and Lester had had a shock. To make wild statements in anger was one thing: to realize clearly how close he had come to murder was another. Lester was through. However, Oorth tried a second time to blackmail the criminal; the conversation between the two was overheard by Miss Ames, who was out skiing. This time, Oorth set a time limit. Knowing that he must kill Oorth, the criminal tried to dispose of Miss Ames by pushing her down the hill under the tractor in case she had recognized his voice. That night he shot and killed Oorth, pulled out his pockets in a search for his medal, but Oorth had turned it over to Mrs. Wheeler for safekeeping."

"You can't blame me for what's happened," Clarisse said shrilly. She clawed at her husband's arm with her long fingernails. "Curtis," she whimpered, "don't just stand there and —"

"Quiet!" Captain Holt warned her.

"Lester, who had come to apologize to Oorth for the near accident, saw the murder committed, and he was warned that no one would believe him, that he and he alone would be regarded as the killer because of the morning's accident with the tree. So Lester ran away into the storm where the murderer fully expected that he would freeze to death from exposure — but where, owing to the loyalty of a fine woman, he was sheltered and saved.''

All this time Don had talked with his head tilted back, his eyes fixed on the wall, one hand resting on Hugh's shoulder. It tightened now as though he were so profoundly weary that he needed support. There was no color in his face, his lips were bloodless.

He ought to be sitting down, Julie thought in alarm. Why does Captain Holt allow him to stand? No one knows how badly he may have been hurt by that blow on the head. Evidently Hugh shared her anxiety, because he turned now to look searchingly at Don, and at what he saw his own color began to fade. No one in the room had stirred. They scarcely seemed to breathe.

To Julie the tension was unbearable. The jaws of the police trap had closed, though she did not yet know whom they had caught. But something had happened in the room. Fear had been let loose.

"That night," Don went on, "our murderer stole the key to the cabin from the nail in the kitchen and ransacked the place, looking for any evidence that Oorth might have against him. The medal, as it happened, had been tossed down beside Oorth's dead body but he had not dared to claim it then and when he returned for his search I had already taken it.

"Miss Ames was attracted by the light and looked out of her window. Once more the murderer tried to get at her, for fear that she had seen him, as he had feared before that she would know his voice. Fortunately" — for the first time Don's voice was husky, faltered a little — "her door was locked."

"You didn't tell me," Mrs. Blaine cried out, and Julie knelt beside her, clasping her cold hand.

"I wasn't hurt," she said. "Just frightened."

Don's voice was getting strained and at a gesture from Captain Holt the ex-houseman brought him a glass of water. He sipped it and went on.

"The next night Carrie arranged to take food to Lester, and the murderer overhead Jul — Miss Ames warn me of the fact.

He followed Carrie in an attempt to find Lester and silence him permanently. Carrie shouted a warning to Lester, who got away. The man struck her down. Because Miss Ames was so close behind, he had no opportunity to mislead us by making false tracks into the woods, so he doubled back, protected by the darkness, and joined us as we came along.

"By this time, you see, he was in a desperate situation. He had killed Downing and Oorth. Lester, who knew his deadly secret, had escaped freezing, was still at large. And there was someone else —" Again Don stopped to steady his voice. "Miss Ames, who had overheard that whispered threat of Oorth's and his answer, 'I'll kill you first'; Miss Ames, who by sheer accident had seen the light in the cabin when he had searched it. So Miss Ames, too, had to be silenced. In the beginning, he had in mind another method of silencing her; but later the situation changed and he held out her safety as his price to me. I was to give up the search for him or he would dispose of her.

"A note, purporting to be from me, took her to the smithy. What he planned to do with her there we don't know. Perhaps he did not intend to hurt her, just keep her until I capitulated. But as it happened, Lester was hidden at the same spot, and while our man was figuring out how to deal with the situation, I arrived. Before that, I had suspected who the criminal was, because of a careless statement he had made. But now I knew. Because he was the only man absent from the lodge during the time when Miss Ames was at the smithy.

"We brought Lester back with us and used him deliberately — and I am pleased to say, with his permission — as a snare. Captain Holt pretended to call off all his people, but actually the houseman and cook only faked going away and returned to guard the cabin. As soon as he had an excuse, our criminal decided to end the situation. A fake call was arranged from the village to get me out of the house. I was struck down, and Monty was killed. Then the killer tried to enter the cabin to silence Lester permanently and discovered to his chagrin that the place was guarded.

"Lester . . ." At his sharp voice Lester, who had been sagging between his two guards, gave a galvanic start. "Lester," Don said firmly, "whom did you see shoot Oorth? Who drove you out into the blizzard?"

Lester's mouth opened, closed again. He looked around the room from face to face as though seeking an answer to a question. Somewhere he found it. His jaws clamped tight together.

Julie, kneeling beside her aunt, clung to her hand. You can taste fear in this room, she thought, but who is it? Who is it?

Lester shook his head. "I didn't see anyone," he said sullenly.

"Lester!" It was Carrie staggering across the room to him, the nurse holding her arm, supporting her.

"That woman should be in bed," Captain Holt exclaimed. "She's not fit to stand."

"Let her speak," Don said. "She went out tonight to try to save Lester by making him talk. She took a terrible risk, not the first one she has taken for him. I hope he is worthy of it."

Carrie had reached Lester now and at a muttered word from Holt the two guards released his arms, stepped back. She put her shaking hands on his chest.

"Lester," she said, "you've been foolish. You let yourself be deceived and misled; you nearly did a terrible thing. *But you didn't do it,* Lester. Remember that. You didn't do it. If you keep still now, you'll be protecting the man who has terrorized us all —"

Lester spoke slowly. "Did he hurt you much, Carrie?"

It was Don who answered bluntly, "He tried to kill her."

Lester looked down at the trembling woman, smiled suddenly, a smile that brightened his face, bent his head and kissed her cheek, kissed the scar. He straightened up slowly until his head was high, his shoulders squared.

"I'll do whatever you want me to, Carrie," he said with an effort.

"Then tell them the truth, Lester."

"Whatever happens?"

"Whatever happens."

"All right," he said. "I don't know what will happen to me now, but I guess it's been my fault and I deserve what I get. I'm sick and tired of pulling someone else's chestnuts out of the fire. And yet in the beginning it sounded . . ." He looked bewildered. "It sounded fine.

Like a new deal all around for the poor. Like heaven on earth. But that was before I saw Oorth die. It was before I knew I was the fall guy. Before I was scared out of my wits, and half frozen, and half starved. If you want to know who your Communist pal is, it's —''

There was a sudden movement, quickly checked. Don's fingers clamped on Hugh's shoulder. Captain Holt had a revolver in his hand.

''You can't get away, Gordon,'' Don said. ''It's all over.''

''Hugh Gordon,'' the captain intoned, ''I arrest you for the murders of Downing and Oorth and for —''

Gordon stood motionless while he was handcuffed and searched. A good-looking lad with auburn hair and a cleft chin. His eyes were sick with fear. They turned from side to side, seeking for help, for a way out of the trap he had baited so cleverly for someone else.

''Not Hugh!'' Julie cried out, stunned.

He turned to her then, his face working. ''You believe me, don't you, Julie? Tell Bruce. Don't let them hurt me. Don't let them — take me away. They can't do anything to me, can they, Julie? I was just

— I couldn't help —" his voice rose hysterically. "Don't let them, Julie!"

She covered her ears with her hands to shut out his terrified cries. He couldn't believe someone would not come to his rescue.

One of the troopers stepped forward and fastened handcuffs on the shaking man. Then, at last, he knew that he was through.

"You see," he said, still to Julie, "I've never had any luck. Nothing ever went right for me. I never had the things other boys did. I never held a job very long. I never kept my friends. It's all so unfair. I fell in love with you. I thought that if you married me it would be all right; you'd never tell that you knew what I had done. But you were going to marry Bruce, instead. It's always been like that. I didn't want to — hurt you but I had no choice. You see that, don't you? It had to be you or me. I had no choice."

He broke off to ask Don, "What was that careless remark I made? I didn't think I'd made any mistakes."

"You told me about Oorth's pockets being turned inside out and you couldn't have seen that from the doorway. You must have been inside the cabin. So I knew you had lied.''

''And just for that —''

''No,'' Don said, ''that gave me my first suspicion, but there was a great deal more. Chiefly a matter of character. Charlie Keane took torture rather than betray his friends. Wheeler took solitary confinement as the price for trying to escape. Even Oorth didn't sell out. There was only one man who thought life ought to give him things, that he should not have to earn them. Only one man who felt sorry for himself, though both Wheeler and Keane had more bitter problems to solve than you ever faced in your life.''

Don took a deep breath. ''All right, Captain. You can take him away now.''

XX

NEW YORK in April. Fifth Avenue washed clean by a spring rain. Blue skies with soft white clouds scudding through them. Shop windows filled with light dresses and summer suits and small saucy straw hats. A few horseback riders in Central Park. Children sailing toy boats in the little pond, trying out new roller skates, shooting marbles. The balloon man whistling as he strolled along a path in the park, demonstrating his giant balloons to the delight of the youngsters who left their nurses to flock around him.

Julie drew in her breath with quivering delight. She had dreamed of this homecoming from the day she and her Aunt Deb had set out on their trip to Europe, which Newton Brewster had made them take after that last tragic scene at the lodge. After all, he had pointed out, she could well afford it now that she was assured that her husband's estate was safe.

The trip, now that she looked back on it, seemed unreal, a kaleidoscope of pictures from a dream: bathing on the Riviera, art galleries in Florence, sleepy days in Greece, shopping in Paris, parties and more parties in London.

And all the time she had felt exiled. Her reward had come from watching the strain fade out of her aunt's face, the color come back to her skin, the sparkle to her eyes; from knowing that her heart had slowed down, steadied, grown stronger. None the less, it had been a time of waiting.

That morning, hours before the boat was due to dock in New York, she had got up and dressed quietly so as not to disturb her aunt and gone on deck. The air was cold and raw with a white rolling mist. She had leaned against the rail, her coat collar turned up about her ears, hands thrust deep in her pockets, shivering as she tried to peer through the fog. Then slowly the mist had drifted away; the sun shone on bright water, and in the distance, dim at first, appeared the towers of Manhattan, like dream castles, floating without any base. Then the sun was overhead, the mist was gone, and New York stood, magnificent and proud and beautiful. On Julie's left waited the tall white lady with the serene face and the uplifted arm who seemed to be saying, "Welcome home," as she had welcomed so many.

Julie had sighed deep with contentment and gone down to join Aunt Deb for breakfast — and then, before leaving her cabin, had stood for a long time before the mirror, adjusting the tiny French hat at the right angle on her head, studying the exquisite cut of her plain gray suit. Her cheeks seemed unduly flushed, her eyes too bright. She had laughed at that revealing face. "Portrait of a woman in love," she had told her radiant image, and gone on deck to watch the tugs nudge the giant liner into its slip.

Her eyes were on the waiting crowds down below, searching for a tall man with a bronzed face and clear gray eyes, but they did not find him. Instead, they rested on the face of Quentin Harrington, who waved his hat wildly as he caught sight of her and flourished an immense bouquet of white roses.

Julie clutched her aunt's arm. "Oh

dear, Aunt Deb, there's Quentin!''

''I thought,'' Mrs. Blaine said in surprise, ''you made it clear to him when he came up to the lodge'' — her voice trembled as she remembered that terrible night — ''that you were not going to marry him.''

''I did,'' Julie wailed, ''but Quentin never gives up.''

Released by the customs man, they went to meet Quentin, who stood waiting for them. He took Aunt Deb's outstretched hand and then turned to thrust the roses into Julie's arms. While she was occupied with them he bent over and kissed her.

''Julie,'' he began huskily.

''Quentin,'' she said, ''why did you come?''

''I've planned everything around you all my life,'' he said simply. ''I can't seem to make any plans that don't involve you. I hoped —'' He drew her out of the noisy, happy crowd of people welcoming friends and family, pouring out their most urgent news at the tops of their voices.

''You're so lovely,'' he began. ''I've never seen you look like this. Can't we start over, Julie?''

Her eyes filled with tears. "I'm terribly sorry, Quentin. I don't want to hurt you, but it's just no use. I can't marry you — ever."

It was her pity for him rather than her words that convinced him. He lifted her hand to his lips. "All right, Julie. I won't bother you any more. I hope — I hope he deserves you and that you'll be happy; always have that look in your eyes, even if it can't be for me."

He turned abruptly and strode away without a backward look. Julie wiped her eyes and went to join her aunt, who was talking to Newton Brewster's chauffeur as he collected their luggage.

And so they had driven through the April day to the last port of call, the end of the journey. The car drew up before the marble front of Newton Brewster's house and Stamm, who had been on the watch, hastened down the marble steps as fast as his increasing corpulence would permit, to open the door.

"Good afternoon, Stamm."

"Good afternoon, Mrs. Blaine. Miss Ames."

He held the door open for them with a flourish and Newton Brewster came out of his library to welcome them.

"Deborah, my dear!" He took both her hands and stood back to look at her. "Paris was just what you needed. I haven't seen you look so well in years."

"I am well, Newton," she assured him. "Rested and relaxed, with all that nightmare behind me."

"Julie," he said smiling, "you'll be a public menace if you continue to go around looking so infernally attractive."

Julie laughed as she handed the white roses to Stamm. "Paris clothes make the woman," she declared.

"Nonsense, they just adorn her. But come in, come in."

As Julie was about to follow her aunt into the library Brewster's hand on her arm checked her. "Just a minute," he said in a low tone. "I think you have some unfinished business to attend to."

He opened the door of his study and when she had gone inside he closed the door behind her. A tall man with a bronzed face and clear gray eyes rose as she appeared.

"Don!" What made her heart pound so, made her breath come in such quick gasps, made her tremble like this?

He took both her outstretched hands and smiled down at her. ''I simply couldn't wait any longer to talk to you, so Mr. Brewster was merciful and let me come here. There's so much I want to say . . .''

She drew away from him. She'd known, of course, that she would see him as soon as she and Aunt Deb returned from Europe. But, though she had thought of little else, she found she was not quite ready.

''It's wonderful to see you,'' she said quickly, forestalling his eager words. ''Because I want to know what happened after we left.''

There was understanding in his eyes as he smiled down at her. ''There's nothing to be afraid of, my darling,'' he told her gently. ''But sit down instead of hovering as though on the verge of flight and I'll satisfy that curiosity of yours — if I can.''

''If you can?''

''Well, when you look so distractingly pretty, it will be hard to keep my mind on anything but you. First, though, Hugh Gordon, as you know from the papers, is awaiting trial. He talked too much to reporters, trying to justify himself. He seems to feel that even the murders were excusable because Downing and Oorth constituted a threat to his own safety. He thinks luck was against him. You know, Julie,'' and his tone was somber, ''there was a time when I was looking for the woman in the case. Sometimes I wonder if Hugh wouldn't have turned out better if he hadn't been the only child of an unhappy widow who spoiled him and thought he had a right to everything; if she — Well, that's the past now and the harm is done. . . . Who told you,'' his tone changed abruptly, ''that blue was the perfect color for you?''

''Why I — what's going on at the lodge?''

It was difficult to meet his eyes, to see the laughter in them and the tenderness, and something deeper, more disturbing, blazing in their depths — more disturbing because it was so controlled.

''Well, let's see. I could talk better, you know, if I were holding your hand.'' He reached for it, clasped it tightly in his warm one. ''Wheeler took over my place when I left, and from all I hear he is doing a bang-up job; the cutting will be finished in a couple of days and he is going to stay on permanently to manage the lumber camp for your aunt. Clarisse went out to Reno, got a quickie divorce, and the last I heard she was preparing to marry some other poor devil.

"The Keanes came back to New York and then went to Bermuda for a second honeymoon. When they return, Charlie is going to have a job as a news photographer on one of the big papers."

"You arranged that for him," Julie said. "Mr. Brewster wrote Aunt Deb about it."

Still holding her hand firmly he slid his other arm around her shoulders, drew her close to him. "Julie —"

She held him off. "What — what about Lester?"

He laughed, shook her lightly. "Don't you drive a man too far," he warned her with a mock scowl. "Lester is going to be all right. Since Mr. Brewster sent Carrie to a plastic surgeon, the scar has been covered and will hardly show at all in a few months' time. They are going to be married. Lester went like a man to talk to the loggers. He confessed what he had tried to do in stirring them up. Naturally, they were angry, but he had always been popular with them and they are willing to start all over, so long as he behaves himself, and Wheeler has given him back his job on that condition. Though there's nothing to worry about.'' Don laughed softly. ''Carrie will keep him in order from now on.''

Safe in the circle of his arms, Julie tossed off her small hat and rested her head against his shoulder. Don looked down at that nestling head and bent forward so that his cheek rested on the soft near-black curls.

''Wheeler writes me that the village people are rallying around in splendid shape, being helpful and cooperative in every possible way. So all's well, my darling.''

''We owe everything to you,'' Julie said, her voice muffled against his chest. ''Clearing up the murders and making it possible for Aunt Deb to save her estate, and — and saving my life t-twice —''

He lifted her head so that she had to look at him. There was no more escape, no more putting off. The determination in his eyes told her that.

''Now,'' he said, ''I want to know whether you are going to stop running away and stay here where you belong. In fact, I may just chain you up, with a ring around your finger and a sign saying: Mrs. Don Bruce.''

''How can I prevent it?'' Julie said with a tremulous laugh and a look of mock despair. ''Th-they say if someone saves your life it belongs to him.''

''I love you, Julie. I loved you that first moment when I looked across a restaurant and found you. Then you were the love-liest thing I'd ever seen; but now I've discovered how much more you are: loyal and courageous and as true as steel. There's laughter in you and gallantry and a capacity for love. Julie, Julie, could you learn to love me?''

There was no laughter in his gray eyes now, only deep emotion and an anguished question. She forgot everything but his need of her, his need to be secure in her love.

''Oh, Don,'' she whispered, ''I think I learned to love you before I even knew your name.''

His face lighted and he kissed her mouth and her eyes and her cheeks. At length she drew away breathlessly. ''Heavens, I didn't know —''

"That I loved you so much? Remember, I've been waiting months for that kiss."

"Then you needn't — needn't wait any longer." She clasped her arms around his neck.

The door opened and there was a discreet cough. "Mr. Brewster asked me to say that luncheon is served." Stamm's blank expression yielded to a delighted grin. "And may I say — heartiest congratulations to you both."

The publishers hope that this Large
Print Book has brought you pleasurable
reading. Each title is designed to make
the text as easy to see as possible.
G. K. Hall Large Print Books are
available from your library and
your local bookstore. Or you can
receive information on upcoming
and current Large Print Books by
mail and order directly from the
publisher. Just send your name
and address to:

G. K. Hall & Co.
70 Lincoln Street
Boston, Mass. 02111

A note on the text
Large print edition designed by
Cindy Schrom.
Composed in 18 pt Times Roman
on a Merganthaler Linotron 202
by Modern Graphics, Inc.